*And as a token of our thanks for your past custom - please accept this
exclusive copy of Barbara Cartland's exciting new novel ...*

FASCINATION IN FRANCE

FASCINATION IN FRANCE

Lady Celita Dale who was the daughter of the Earl and Countess of Langdale has been at a Finishing School with her great friend Judy.

At the last moment Judy gets a letter from her Father to say that instead of coming back home as they both expected, they are to go with one of the Sisters from the Convent and a Courier, to Arles.

Judy realises that this is because her father who is Lord Waterforde, is exceedingly rich and wishes her to marry the *Duc* de Sahran who lives in Provence.

She is absolutely desperate as she is madly in love with a charming young man called Clive Cunningham, who lives near them in the country.

They have been meeting secretly but Judy dare not tell her Father, as she is quite sure he will not think Clive important enough for her.

Because Judy is so desperate Celita says that she will take Judy's place and so the two girls arriving at the magnificent Château which belongs to the *Duc* change places.

How they find the Château is the most exquisite place they have ever seen, how Celita understands why the *Duc* is worried that he cannot keep it up as it should be and also, as is customary in France, look after his very large family of relations.

How she discovers that Provence is fascinating, exceedingly beautiful and is intrigued by the famous Gorges, and how eventually after a dangerous situation caused by one of the *Duc*'s previous love affairs, the whole puzzle is solved in this unusual 513th novel by **BARBARA CARTLAND**.

BARBARA CARTLAND

Fascination
in France

First published in Great Britain 1993
by J. D. Williams Group Ltd.,
53 Dale Street,
Manchester M60 6ES

Copyright © Cartland Promotions 1993

ISBN 1 898619 00 X

Phototypeset by Intype, London
Printed and bound in Great Britain by
BPCC Paperbacks Ltd.,
Tring Road,
Aylesbury, Bucks.

AUTHOR'S NOTE

I visited Provence at Easter 1990, and realised what an exquisitely beautiful part of France it is.

The tiny villages perched upon craggy cliffs, the gaily coloured harbours with their fishing boats, the fantastic gorges with their thousand foot drops on either side in the cascading water left me breathless.

I was also thrilled with the legends which are part of every town and village and are part of the ancient little Abbeys half hidden amidst trees, and magnificent palaces once inhabited by Popes.

There is a mystery about Provence which is difficult to put into words but it remains with one, long after one has left France, and makes sure that having once visited this fascinating and very different province one is compelled to return.

Chapter One
1878

Celita packed the last of her books, then looked around the room to see if she had forgotten anything.

It was quite a small room but she had made it very comfortable while she was at the finishing school.

In a way she was sad to leave it, with all her books close at hand and the prizes she had won arranged on the mantelpiece.

She walked to the window and looked out over the garden.

It was most attractive with the spring flowers in bloom and the pale green leaves on the trees.

The aristocratic Seminary for Young Ladies was just outside Paris.

While Celita was there she had never been allowed to see any of the festivities of Paris which were talked about by everyone in England.

Instead she was taken to the museums, the picture galleries and the churches.

At the same time she was always conscious of the gaiety and frivolity of Paris in the air!

One did not actually have to take part in it to feel it.

"One day," she told herself, "when I am older, I would like to come back to Paris and enjoy the theatres and restaurants and all the other entertainments which are apparently more amusing here than anywhere else in Europe."

Of course they were whispered about at the School!

The other girls, a fair number of whom were French, had dashing brothers.

Even some of their fathers enjoyed what were very special amusements designed especially for men.

Celita, however, had spent her time at school learning everything she could.

She was well aware that her mother had made many sacrifices so that she could be properly educated.

The Dowager Countess of Langdale had been left a widow two years ago.

Celita had thought at the time that her mother would never recover from the loss of her husband.

Yet because the Countess was a sensible, as well as a very beautiful woman, she had thought of her daughter.

She forced herself to lay aside her black and concentrate on Celita's education.

"I am afraid, Darling," she said, "now Papa is dead we shall be very poor, as all the money of course goes to the new Earl. I shall not be able to give you a Ball as we had wanted to do, but at least you will be able to share Judy's."

"I understand that, Mama," Celita said, "and you must not worry yourself about me. When I am a débutante I shall be perfectly happy as long as I am able to ride Lord Waterforde's horses and be with you here in our home."

It was in fact a very attractive house.

Lord Waterforde, to whom it belonged, had begged the fourth Earl of Langdale to come and live on his estate.

He had realised that Langdale Hall, the family house, had become too heavy a financial burden for him.

The Hall was, in fact, not only extremely large and expensive to keep up but really not a very attractive house.

The Earl and Countess had therefore been delighted with the small Elizabethan house which Lord Waterforde had offered them.

They had been extremely happy there with Celita, their only child.

A large part of their happiness derived from the fact that Lord Waterforde, who was very wealthy, owned a fine stable of horses.

The Earl was an expert breeder, as well as being one of the outstanding riders in the country.

"I need your help," Lord Waterforde had said. "Why do you go on killing yourself to keep that huge and uncomfortable pile open, when you know it costs you every penny you possess?"

This was sheer common sense.

The Earl had therefore thankfully closed Langdale Hall and moved into Four Gables.

"It will be lovely to be home with Mama," Celita was telling herself now.

She was also seeing the sleek, well-bred and spirited horses which filled Lord Waterforde's stables.

She would race Judy on them over the flat land every morning before breakfast.

As if thinking of Judy had conjured her up, the door burst open and Judy Forde came running in.

"Celita! Celita!" she cried. "I have had a .. letter from Papa – I cannot bear it .. I .. cannot."

There was no mistaking the distress and anguish in Judy's voice.

Celita turned quickly from the window to ask:

"What has happened? What is wrong?"

"It is Papa .. we are .. not to go .. home tomorrow as planned . . . but to go and stay with the *Duc* de Sahran."

Celita stared at her friend.

Judy was a very pretty girl.

But now there were tears in her eyes and an expression of anguish on her face.

It was very disturbing.

"I cannot understand, Dearest," Celita said. "Come and sit down and explain to me all about it."

"I was always .. afraid of .. this," Judy answered. "When we were home last holidays I was quite certain Papa was planning that I should marry someone .. important just because .. I will have so much .. money."

She paused before she went on tearfully:

"You know .. I want to .. marry Clive .. you know I .. love him .. Oh, Celita! What .. shall I .. do?"

Celita put her hand up to her forehead and then said quietly:

"Start at the beginning, Dearest. I cannot understand what you are saying and why we cannot go home tomorrow as planned."

"I know .. I know!" Judy answered. "Sister Agnes was to .. accompany us to .. Dover, where Papa .. said he would .. meet us."

Celita nodded, she knew all this.

Lord Waterforde had always made extremely precise arrangements when they travelled.

They were invariably accompanied by either a Nun or a Chaperon of some sort besides a Courier.

When they were in England there was also a footman to attend to their luggage.

It had been arranged last holidays that when they left at the end of this term, the two girls would travel together as usual.

It certainly made things very much easier for the Countess, and also, which was a serious consideration, it was much cheaper.

"Leave everything to me," Lord Waterforde would say.

The Countess was very grateful to be able to do so.

"What has your father written to you?" Celita enquired in a quiet voice.

"He says," Judy answered with a gulp, "that instead of going home we are to .. go with Sister Agnes .. and the Courier to .. Arles."

"To Arles!" Celita exclaimed. "In Provence?"

"Yes," Judy answered. "That is where the *Duc* de Sahran lives."

"And we are to stay with him?" Celita enquired.

She was trying to get the story straight.

It all sounded incredible.

To have everything changed at the very last minute was, to say the least of it, disturbing.

"I do .. not want to .. meet the *Duc*," Judy declared. "I know exactly .. why Papa is .. sending us there, and I .. hate him .. already. Do you hear Celita? I hate him!"

"How can you hate someone you have never met?" Celita objected. "Why do you hate him?"

"Because Papa is planning that I should .. marry him, and I do not .. want to be .. married to a .. *Duc*. I might have .. guessed that is what he has been .. trying to .. concoct."

Celita looked at her friend enquiringly.

Judy went on.

"Last holidays Papa .. talked to me about .. my future and .. he said:

" 'I hope, dearest, you will marry someone with whom you will be very happy. But you must understand that I want him to be someone of importance.'

" 'Why, Papa?' " I asked.

"Papa replied: 'You will be very rich, perhaps extremely rich, so I have no wish for you to be pursued by fortune-hunters and ne're-do-well young men who have lost everything they possess at the card-tables.'

"I told him I could understand that," Judy said, "but also that I wanted to be in love with the man I marry."

"And what did your father say to that?" Celita enquired.

"He said: 'Of course! Of course!' It is the way he speaks when he is brushing something I have said aside."

Judy looked up at Celita and her voice broke as she went on:

"I wanted to .. tell him then that I .. love Clive, but .. I knew it .. would be a .. mistake. And .. now, if I am .. not .. careful, I shall be .. rushed up the aisle with this .. *Duc* and perhaps .. never see .. Clive again."

Tears fell down her cheeks as she finished speaking and Celita put her arms round her.

She knew only too well that her friend had been in love with Clive Cunningham for over a year.

He was a charming and handsome young man who lived in

Berkshire and whom they regularly met when they were out riding.

At first it had been by chance, and then because he had fallen in love with Judy, he turned up every morning.

He also made many assignations to meet her in Celita's home.

He was quite obviously head-over-heels in love and Judy loved him.

Celita had however been afraid that Lord Waterforde would not think him good enough for his daughter.

His Lordship was very conscious of his huge fortune.

Most of it he had made by using his own intelligence, investing in the right shares at the right time.

Besides, of course, being in contact with the right people.

Because he had no son and there was no heir to the title, Judy would inherit everything he possessed.

Celita had often thought that Lord Waterforde would have set his sights on the Prince of Wales as a son-in-law if he were not already married.

In fact Lord Waterforde would think nothing less than a Duke was good enough for Judy.

But Celita had certainly not expected it would be a French Duke.

Now she asked while Judy cried on her shoulder:

"What do you know about the *Duc* de Sahran?"

"The girls here . . have talked about . . him," Judy said after a moment's hesitation. "He is always giving . . parties in . . Paris to which their brothers go but no . . real ladies are . . invited."

For a moment Celita looked puzzled and Judy explained:

"He entertains . . the coquettes! The women who drive in the Bois . . covered in glittering jewels, and whose . . dogs have collars of . . real diamonds and emeralds!"

Celita laughed.

"How ridiculous! I am sure the dogs, if they are proper dogs, would not appreciate such collars."

"One of the women has her .. poodles dyed the same colour as .. her dresses," Judy said.

Celita laughed again.

"Well if that is the sort of woman the *Duc* likes, he will not be interested in you."

"He will be .. interested in .. my money," Judy said, "so that he can .. afford to buy .. jewelled dog-collars."

"I do not believe it," Celita declared. "The whole thing is ridiculous! Your father cannot really expect you to marry such a silly man."

"But he does! I am sure that .. he intends me to .. marry .. the *Duc*" Judy sobbed.

"Then you must refuse him," Celita said.

Judy raised her head from her friends's shoulder.

"I shall not .. be allowed to .. do that," she said, "I know now .. why Papa .. pointed out to me last holidays that .. a Father can .. choose the man his daughter .. marries."

She gave another sob as she said:

"I thought .. Papa was being .. funny, and I said: 'If you choose .. the King of Siam .. for me, I shall .. run away'."

"What did your father say to that?" Celita asked.

"He said, 'I do not want you to sit on the throne of Siam, and I promise you, my Dearest, that any husband I choose for you will be exactly the right man to look after you and protect you'."

"Well the *Duc* does not sound the sort of man your father was thinking of," Celita observed.

"But we have .. to go and .. stay with him at his .. Château, and I am quite .. quite certain that when I am .. there, I will .. find myself .. caught into an .. engagement and then .. there will be .. no escape."

As she finished speaking, Judy burst into more floods of tears.

She put her handkerchief up to her eyes.

Holding her in her arms, Celita was wondering what she could do.

She had always suspected that Lord Waterforde, who was a

great snob, would try to find someone very important for his only daughter to marry.

But she had not expected him to do anything until Judy had 'come out' as a débutante.

Then there would be the Ball in London he had promised her, and also, even more exciting, the Ball in the country.

Lord Waterforde had already talked it over with Lady Langdale.

He knew she would have as many people as possible to stay at Four Gables.

He had also arranged with their other neighbours that every house would be packed with his guests.

There were to be two orchestras, one of which was a gypsy band which had already become famous in London.

At the end of the evening fireworks would be let off over the lake.

"It will be thrilling, Mama, I know it will be thrilling," Celita said to her mother.

"I am sure it will be, Dearest," the Countess agreed. "I feel it will be your Ball as much as Judy's, since you do everything together."

"At least we shall have all our special friends there," Celita said thinking of Clive Cunningham, "while in London Lord Waterforde will be entertaining people none of us know."

"That is true," the Countess said, "and I am making you a very special gown which you can wear at both Balls."

Judy's gowns were to come from the most expensive shop in Bond Street.

Celita knew her mother's taste was impeccable and she had made her gowns ever since she was a small child.

She would be able to aspire to being 'the Belle of the Ball', while Judy would be the Shining Star of it.

Now it seemed as if Lord Waterforde had changed his plans just because he wanted Judy to be a Duchess.

Celita loved Judy and she was in fact exactly like a sister to her.

She wondered desperately how she could help her.

Finally she said aloud:

"Now, listen, Dearest, it is no use looking on the black side of things until we are quite certain your Father intends this to happen and there is no hope of your being able to escape."

"I know it will happen," Judy wailed. "I know Papa wants me to be a Duchess! He will never let me be just Mrs. Cunningham."

Clive Cunningham's father was, in fact, the fifth Baronet of a most distinguished family.

But Celita had to admit that hardly compared with the *Duc* of Sahran, and Clive, being only the second son, was not even heir to the Baronetcy.

Now that she thought about him, she seemed to have heard that his Château was outstanding.

He had, someone had told her, many remarkable treasures which had survived the Revolution.

At the same time she had not listened, as apparently Judy had, to the stories the other girls had to tell about him.

There were fifty girls in the school, all coming from distinguished families in different parts of Europe.

It was not surprising there was a good deal of gossip.

Inevitably as the girls grew older and it would be only a few months before they left school, they talked about the men they would meet.

They were well aware which names were on their mother's list of eligible bachelors.

The Countess had never made such a list.

"I married your father," she said, "because he fell in love with me, and I with him. He was not the Earl in those days, and I promise you I was not the slightest bit influenced by thinking of how important he would be "

Her voice softened as she added:

"I just loved him because he was the most handsome man I had ever seen."

"And he loved you, Mama, because you were so beautiful," Celita replied. "He told me once that you shone like a star at

15

every party at which he met you, and it was impossible for him to see any other woman."

For a moment the Countess's eyes were misty and then she said:

"I miss him desperately, Darling, but now I have to think of you, hoping that you will find someone like Papa and know he is the right man for you and that you would never be happy with anyone else."

"That is exactly what I want," Celita said.

Looking at her daughter the Countess knew a great number of men would fall in love with her.

Not only was Celita very lovely but her beauty was somehow different from that of most English girls.

Her hair was very fair and her skin the traditional perfect pink and white.

But she had something more.

A personality which seemed to impress itself almost immediately on anyone who met her.

It was difficult, the Countess thought, to put it into words.

But Celita had a spiritual look which was missing in most young women, especially those who appeared in London society.

The Countess prayed very fervently that her daughter would know the same happiness that she had been granted and would never be disillusioned.

"What are we to do? What are we to do?" Judy was asking now.

"We will have to go and stay with the *Duc* as your father has arranged," Celita answered. "But we must also try to prevent him from proposing to you."

"Perhaps he will just fix it up with Papa," Judy said miserably.

"I cannot believe any man who was a man would do that," Celita said. "It would be insulting if the *Duc* did not ask you to be his wife himself. In any case we cannot be certain that is what he does intend."

"He intends it all right," Judy insisted. "Papa implies it in his letter."

She looked down at it, where it was lying rather crumpled on her knee.

"He says: '*I have met the Duc on various race-courses and found him a most interesting and intelligent young man. He is a good judge of horses, which I like in any man. I would enjoy helping him expand his stables as he wishes to do.*' Why can he not expand them himself?" Judy asked as she finished reading.

Celita knew the answer to that, but she did not say so aloud.

The *Duc* obviously needed money, and who had more money to spend than Lord Waterforde?

"I am afraid," she said, "we shall have to go the the Château, dearest, but perhaps we need not stay long. Is your father coming out to meet us there?"

"No, Papa says he cannot do that immediately. My Aunt Mabel, whom I have never liked, is to meet us as soon as we arrive. I am quite certain she will be pushing me into the *Duc's* arms."

Celita, who had met Judy's aunt and found her an unattractive woman, thought this was more than likely.

Lady Hilton was the widow of a man who had been much older than she was.

Since she was widowed she had spent a great deal of time with her brother, seeking, Celita rather expected, another husband.

As she was a rather tiresome and pushy woman, she had so far failed in her search.

Celita could not help thinking it was a pity that she would be at the Château, for she was certain to upset Judy.

"Try not to worry, dearest," she said to her friend. "It is no use crying until you have to. I am quite certain we can find some way out of this predicament."

"What way out can there possibly be?" Judy asked in a voice of gloom. "The *Duc* wants my money, Papa wants me to be a Duchess, and Aunt Mabel wants any crumbs that fall from a rich man's table."

Celita laughed because she could not help it.

"Now you are beginning to see the funny side of it," she said. "and that is very sensible of you, Dearest."

"I do not think it is at all funny," Judy said. "I want to marry Clive, I love Clive, and I am going to write and tell him so."

"He knows it already," Celita said. "I am just wondering whether it would help if he told your father that he desperately wants to marry you."

"We advised him not to do so last holidays," Judy reminded her. "We thought then it was too soon, and now it is too late."

"Nothing is too late until you are actually walking down the aisle with the *Duc*," Celita declared. "What we have to do is somehow to find a way out, and I have a feeling in my bones that we will manage it."

"Do you really feel that?" Judy asked in a serious tone. "Or are you just saying it to make me happier?"

"I really do believe it," Celita assured her. "I am certain I shall think of something before we reach the Château which will convince the *Duc* that he does not want to marry you."

"Only one thing would convince him of that: to hear that Papa had lost all his money," Judy said.

"That would be a disaster anyway," Celita replied. "Think how horrible it would be if he had to sell Waterforde Court and you could not have your Ball."

"No, I shall have my Ball," Judy said miserably, "and Papa will arrange for my engagement to be announced on the same day. I know exactly how his mind works. He will think that would be an appropriate occasion."

"In that case we have a little time to make sure he does nothing of the sort," Celita said. "We have just got to pray for a miracle to happen to save you, and somehow I am sure there will be one."

"Oh, I hope so," Judy sighed. "I am frightened, so very

18

frightened, that I shall lose Clive and find myself married to the *Duc*, far away from you and everyone else."

"I can understand your feeling like that," Celita said, "but it does not help. You are yielding to your emotions at the moment, and we must concentrate on our brains."

She raised her hand to her forehead as she added:

"Think, Judy, think what we can do! That is the only way we can save you."

"I doubt it," Judy answered. But she wiped her eyes.

. . . .

The two girls set off for their journey by train.

Sister Agnes and Judy's lady's-maid were sitting on the small seat of the carriage facing the back of the train.

There had been a great many "Goodbyes" to say.

The School-mistress had made a speech at the supper last night.

She had said how much she would miss both the Hon. Judy Forde and Lady Celita Dale when the next term started.

"You have both been outstandingly good pupils," she said, "and I am very proud to have had you in my school. I shall look forward to hearing what happens to you now that you are going out into the world, and I feel sure that the report will be one of happiness."

Every girl present knew what the School-mistress meant by that.

It was that Celita and Judy would be married to distinguished and important men.

In her private sitting-room, there were a large number of photographs of girls who had left the school.

The majority, in ornate silver frames, were of their weddings attended by elegant bridesmaids and small pages.

Celita could not help thinking a little cynically that if Judy married the *Duc* she would have a place of honour in the collection.

If it was merely Clive, she might not even have her picture framed.

"It is all social snobbery," she told herself. "I just hope I can find someone like Papa, even if just a plain Mister, and we can live in a nice little house in the country and have lots of dogs and at least four children."

Then she laughed to herself.

For the moment she had to struggle with the problem of Judy and whether or not she was to marry the *Duc*.

If they had been going to England, taking the train from the *Gare de Nord* to Calais, a first-class compartment would have been reserved for the two young ladies and Sister Agnes, and the one next door for the Courier and Judy's lady's-maid.

But for the much longer journey to Arles from the *Gare de Lyon* a private coach had been attached for them to the express.

It was a special concession that Judy had been allowed to have a lady's-maid at school. Then only the promise that Martha should also do what she could for the other girls.

This had been agreed, but Celita was aware that, after looking after Judy, Martha did as little as possible for anyone else except herself.

"They should have their own maids with them," Martha said firmly.

"I am sure in most cases, like me, they cannot afford them," Celita objected.

"You're different, M'Lady," Martha explained. "I likes looking after you, your clothes are real beautiful, the way Her Ladyship makes them."

"Mama is very clever," Celita agreed. "And I am so lucky that you take care of her things, which I often tell her should be put in museums."

Martha laughed at this.

But Celita knew she took special trouble pressing and mending her clothes before she took them home for the holidays.

In the train the girls talked to Sister Agnes.

She was an elderly nun who had entered the Convent which adjoined the school because the man she loved had been killed fighting for France.

"Do you ever regret, Sister Agnes," Celita had asked her once, "giving up the world outside and living in a Convent?"

The Sister had taken a little time to reply.

Then she said:

"I often think I would like to have had children, but there was only one man for me, and if I could not have him, then I had to be content with God."

It seemed to Celita a reasonable way of looking at things.

At the same time she told herself she wanted to live and she wanted to see the world.

There was so much to do, so much to enjoy, so much to learn.

Now as the miles passed Judy became more and more depressed.

"I want to go to England," she said. "I hate having to stay in France."

"I know, Dearest," Celita said. "Perhaps we will not have to stay long."

She caught Judy's eye, and they were both thinking it was a question of how long the *Duc* took to propose.

Alternatively, how long it took them to persuade him that, contrary to whatever Lord Waterforde had said, she would not marry him.

"It is going to be difficult – very difficult," Celita admitted to herself.

She tried wildly to think of some excuse for changing their minds at the last minute and going to England as had originally been intended.

Because he was aware how difficult things were for the Countess since her husband's death, fruit from the garden, eggs, chickens and young lambs from the farm came to Four Gables regularly.

When he called on them, which he did frequently, he sometimes left a case of champagne in the Hall.

Or he brought in some special delicacy from London.

"You are too generous," the Countess often said.

"But I enjoy being generous to you," Lord Waterforde asserted. "I cannot say that of everyone on whom I bestow any favours."

"I am sure no one could be ungrateful for all you do for them," the Countess answered.

"You would be surprised," he said. "My relatives take it as a matter of course that I should pay their bills, indulge their extravagances, and, when they require it, supply them with a new house, carriage, horses and anything else they fancy."

Because there was a hard note in his voice, the Countess had put her hand on his arm.

"Do not allow yourself to get cynical," she said. "You know as well as I do that everyone envies a rich man, and nothing is worse than a rich man who is stingy! No one could ever say that of you."

Lord Waterforde had laughed.

"Now you are flattering me and I am enjoying it," he said. "But when people call on me, I find myself wondering how quickly they are going to ask me for something, and I watch them fidgeting around the subject until they can get it out."

"You are not to think like that!" the Countess protested.

"But if you were in my shoes you would think exactly the same," Lord Waterforde said. "Believe it or not, this world is full of spongers. Some have blue eyes and a pathetic story of ill treatment, others are fat and red-nosed and have lost a packet on the Derby!"

Now the Countess, as well, was laughing at his joke, yet they both knew that fortunately it was true.

"We must be very careful not to impose on him," the Countess had often said to Celita.

"Of course not, Mama, but I know that he really loves us, and when you love people you want to give them things."

At the same time, Celita was well aware that His Lordship

could be hard, even cruel, if people disobeyed or obstructed him.

She wanted to help Judy because Judy meant so much to her.

She wanted Judy's happiness as much as she wanted her own.

Nevertheless she knew it would be injurious to her mother if she made an enemy of him.

"If only Papa were here," she sighed. "He was so wise and so sensible, and I am sure he would have known how to handle this very difficult problem."

The train was getting near to Arles and Sister Agnes, who knew the country well, was talking about the City.

She was telling them that they must see some of the gold work for which the artisans of Arles in the past had been famous.

Celita thought this sounded interesting.

She also remembered that the Empress Eugénie had chosen Arles as her residence in Provence, and that there were many ancient Roman remains there, including the palace of the Emperor Constantine the Great.

"There is so much to see," Sister Agnes said enthusiastically. "And it not only has a rich and glorious past, but the air one breathes creates joy and a happy atmosphere."

Celita smiled.

She understood exactly what Sister Agnes was saying.

She had thought ever since she had been in France, that there was a special lilt in the air which made her understand why the French talked of *joie de vivre*.

Judy sat in silence until Sister Agnes had finished speaking and then she said:

"I hate France, I want to go back to England very quickly."

Because she thought it was a mistake for Judy to be so miserable in front of Sister Agnes, Celita changed the subject.

They talked of other things until they arrived at Arles.

There were two very grand carriages, each drawn by four horses and with smart footmen on the box, waiting for them.

The Station-master had been informed of their arrival and escorted them to the carriages.

Then Sister Agnes had to say "Goodbye" to them as she was returning to Paris.

The Station-master promised to see she was comfortably looked after until the Paris train arrived.

The two girls kissed her "Goodbye".

"I will pray for you," Sister Agnes said in a soft voice.

"Please do that," Celita said. "We need your prayers very much at the moment, and will be most grateful for them."

Sister Agnes smiled at her.

"You will always be all right, Celita," she said. "Nothing can keep you down, you mark my words."

Celita laughed.

"Thank you again, Sister. I hope that is true."

Judy got into the carriage and Celita joined her.

The Courier and the lady's-maid with the luggage were to follow them.

"Now we are here," Celita said as they drove off, "you must try to cheer up. There are lots of exciting things to see, so let us forget the *Duc* for a moment and enjoy ourselves."

"How can I enjoy myself," Judy asked, "when I want to go home to Clive? Oh, Celita I ought to have told you before. I begged him to come out to see me and pretend he had come to see you."

"Why did you do that?" Celita said. "That is sure to complicate things, and your father will be angry if he finds out."

"Not if he thinks Clive is pursuing *you*," Judy pointed out.

Celita sighed.

She could see a great many difficulties about all this.

She really had no wish to be in the centre of them.

But she must protect Judy.

She was well aware that Judy had a simple and uncomplicated nature.

Having fallen in love with Clive, she had no wish for anyone else, and just wanted to be allowed to marry him.

Celita could understand how a girl could be swept away by

the excitement of coming out: the Balls, the money spent on her appearance, and the fact that almost anything that she wanted in the world could be hers.

But Judy wanted just one thing, and that was Clive.

It was going to be almost impossible to persuade her even to consider an alternative.

Yet Celita was well aware how furious Lord Waterforde would be if his plans went awry from the very beginning.

The difficulty was she had no idea what she could do.

How could she possibly save Judy from having her heart broken and her future life ruined?

It was all a question of money.

If the *Duc* really wanted money, it would be difficult for him to find anyone richer than Judy.

Celita knew that her father's friends had often made jokes about the enormous wealth Lord Waterforde possessed.

Living on his estate must be like sitting at "the throne of Midas" they had suggested.

"Does he make you feel humble?" one man had inquired.

"Not in the slightest," the Earl replied. "He is one of the most charming and good-tempered men I know, and he never boasts about his money."

"He doesn't need to," another of the Earl's friends retorted sarcastically, "while I am continually counting mine and finding it missing."

They all laughed at that.

But Celita had realised as she listened that they were all envious of Lord Waterforde and resented his being so rich.

She had heard so often how his fortune had accumulated.

How clever he had been in handling it, and how his wife had also been the daughter of a rich man.

"Money goes to money," Celita's old Nanny had remarked, and that indeed was true.

"It can also make people very unhappy," she thought, and looked at Judy.

Judy was staring out of the window, her lips drooping, her eyes filled with misery.

"It is not fair," Celita told herself.

If Judy had already enjoyed a Season in London it might have been different.

But to go straight from school to cope with a man who wanted her money to spend on improper women was too much for anyone so young and inexperienced.

Because Celita was exceedingly intelligent and very well read, she did not feel immature or nervous about entering a new world.

When Lord Waterforde gave his huge parties at the Court, Judy had usually been sent to the school-room.

Or she went to Celita's home until the party was over.

But when friends came to see Celita's Father and Mother, she was always present too.

They might be talking about horses, politics or international affairs.

Her Father was an expert on all of these subjects.

Celita was able to follow what was being said and found it extremely interesting.

It was because of this and what she had learnt at school that she felt in many ways she was very much older than Judy and much more experienced.

"I have to look after her," she told herself. "She will get swallowed up by all the things which are not important instead of concentrating on those that are."

It was difficult however to persuade herself that getting married was not the most important thing of all.

That was exactly what Lord Waterforde had sprung on his daughter the very day of leaving school.

Chapter Two

The *Duc* de Sahran drove down the *Champs Élysèes* with an expertise and a flourish which was the envy of his contemporaries.

He was well aware that his open Chaise was more up-to-date and noticeable than any others moving in the same direction.

His horses also were superlative.

His groom sitting with crossed arms wore livery which was smarter than the liveries of all the other aristocrats.

He had been quite young when he decided he expected perfection in everything and most of all in his Château in Provence.

He had inherited his father's title when he was only 21.

From the moment he had set out to have everything around him as perfect as was possible to find in an imperfect world.

Being extremely intelligent, he knew he was the envy of his friends and a source of fury to his enemies.

It did not trouble him that a large number of people disliked him, but his real friends were very precious.

That he was talked about was something to be expected, especially as he was also extremely handsome.

Ever since he had left school, women had fallen into his arms even before he asked their names.

The result had inevitably made him somewhat cynical.

He was well aware that if he had been a poor man with no prospects he would have had to struggle very much harder.

Yet he was sure he would have attained what he desired in life – nothing less than perfection.

When he reached *La Place de la Concorde*, he deliberately drove around it twice before moving into the *Rue de Rivoli*.

It always gave him enormous satisfaction to look at the beauty of it.

To remember also that it had been *La Place de la Revolution*, from which his family had escaped.

They had saved their lives, but what infuriated him whenever he thought about it was that the Château had been looted.

This was a bitter blow because the revolutionary trend had not been so violent in Provence as in other parts of France.

Many treasures which had been collected by his ancestors over the years – and the Sahrans were one of the oldest families in France – had been lost.

The rag-tag and bobtail who burst into the Château when there was no one there to protect it, stole everything on which they could lay their hands.

The *Duc* had poured over the diaries written by his ancestors.

He had also gone very carefully through the catalogues made by the different generations.

There were so many pieces missing that he had set out to find as many of them as possible.

He had, in fact, succeeded better than his fondest hopes.

This success had increased, even exaggerated his desire to get his own way.

It had certainly strengthened his determination which those who worked for him said "was as stiff as an iron bar".

In fact once he had made up his mind it was very difficult to persuade him to change it in any way.

Apart from these rather unusual aspects of his character, he was kind and exceedingly generous.

He was considerate to those who worked for him, and was known in Provence as an outstandingly good Land-owner and employer.

After his second drive round *La Place de la Concorde* he turned into the *Rue de Rivoli*.

Then he turned again to move towards the *Place Vendôme*.

He stopped outside the shop of one of the famous jewellers and handed the reins to the groom who accompanied him.

Inside he was treated with respect and by the female assistants, with looks of open admiration.

It was well-known that the *Duc* had given some outstanding jewellery to women who enjoyed his favours.

The jewellers of Paris competed with one another to attract his custom.

The Manager of the shop hurried to show him some pieces which had just been completed.

Also some in older settings which they had recently bought.

The *Duc* looked at them with interest.

Finally he chose a very attractive brooch with diamonds and pearls set in the shape of snowdrops.

"I felt certain that would attract your attention, *Monsieur le Duc*," the shop-manager said. "It is from one of our new, young designers who has ideas of his own and will, I think, in the future go far."

"I agree with you," the *Duc* said.

He waited while the brooch was packed in an elegant pink velvet box which was covered with tissue paper and tied with a bow of satin ribbon.

It was the way he always had his gifts packed.

The ribbon was kept under the counter so that it was always at hand when he needed it.

The *Duc* was shown out of the shop.

He got into his Chaise and drove back into the *Rue de Rivoli*.

It was a small house, standing back a little from the others, at which he was calling. '

Again he left his groom in charge of his horses.

Carrying his parcel he went through the outer gate and down a paved path to the front door of the house.

It was opened before he knocked, by a servant who had been told to expect him and was therefore on the alert.

The *Duc* swept off his tall hat, and as the servant curtsied he said:

"Good afternoon, Térèse. Is your Mistress expecting me?"

"Madame is in the Drawing-Room, *Monsieur le Duc*," Térèse answered.

The *Duc* walked lightly up the narrow staircase to the small Reception room which occupied most of the first floor.

It was well furnished and the pictures which had been a present to its owner were valuable.

There was however something slightly flamboyant about the curtains and the upholstery of the sofas and chairs.

The whole room however made a fitting background for its owner, Madame Yvonne Bédoin, who was one of the best known women in Paris.

She was waiting for the *Duc*, reclining on a sofa and leaning back against a number of satin cushions.

They made a perfect frame with their soft eau-de-nil for the darkness of her hair and the translucent white of her skin.

She was wearing a chiffon négligée which did little to disguise the exquisite curves of her body.

When the *Duc* appeared in the doorway, Yvonne held out her arms.

"I was waiting for you, René," she cried. "I was half afraid you had forgotten."

"How could I forget anything so important?" the *Duc* answered with a touch of mockery in his voice.

He crossed the room unhurriedly and taking her hands kissed first one then the other.

He then laid in her lap the present he had bought in the *Place Vendôme*.

Yvonne looked at it then up at the *Duc* through her long, heavily mascarrad eyelashes.

"A present for me?" she asked in a soft seductive voice. "You are so kind, and as you can see I am wearing the necklace you gave me."

The *Duc* glanced at the necklace of diamonds and pearls.

He realised as he did so that the décolletage of its owner was very low.

"I am thrilled to have your present," Yvonne said, "but at the same time I feel rather neglected that you have not been to see me for so long."

"I have been in England," the *Duc* said. "I went over to see my horse run in one of their classic races."

"And of course he won," Yvonne cooed.

"Of course," the *Duc* agreed.

He sat down, not on the sofa beside her as she had expected.

She had moved her legs so that there was room for him, but he chose the nearest chair.

He leant back as he watched her open his present.

She gave a little cry of pleasure.

"Oh, thank you, thank you," she said. "I know who designed this. It will look delightful with my necklace."

"That is what I thought," said the *Duc*, "and it completes the set with your ring."

"You think of everything," Yvonne said. "There was never a man like you."

"That is what I want to believe," the *Duc* said. "Now I have something to tell you which you may find a surprise."

Yvonne put down the brooch she was holding in her hand and gave him a piercing glance.

She knew him well enough to recognise that when he spoke in that determined tone he was planning something.

She was half afraid of what it might be.

"When I was in England," the *Duc* went on. "I had a long talk with Lord Waterforde, who is a well-known racehorse-owner and won the Gold Cup at Ascot last year."

"Horses, always horses," Yvonne murmured. "I was hoping when you were away that you were thinking of me."

She spoke very softly and there was an invitation in her eyes which most men found irresistible.

The *Duc*, sitting back in his chair, was not looking directly at her but staring ahead of him.

"It was after I had discussed several matters with Lord Waterforde," he said, "including our horses, that I made a decision I have never made before."

'And what was that?" Yvonne enquired.

"I intend to get married."

If the *Duc* had dropped a bomb and it had exploded, blowing off the ceiling of the drawing-room, it could not have caused greater consternation.

Yvonne sat up on the sofa and stared at him.

"You have – decided to – get – married?"

There was a shrill note in her voice which had not been there before.

"That is what I said," he replied, "and that is what I intend to do."

"But why, why? It is something you have never considered before. In fact you said you would never marry after what happened when you were little more than a boy."

The *Duc* frowned because this was something he had no wish to remember.

He had been little over 19 when his father, in the way that was usual in France, had arranged for his marriage to the daughter of another *Duc*.

She had a large Dowry, which was not of particular interest to young René de Sahran, and he had no wish at all to be married.

Having left school, he was enjoying the delights of Paris where the most seductive and beautiful women in Europe were to be found.

He was young, handsome and rich.

Who could ask for more?

There were nights of wild gaiety which only ended when the sun had risen.

There were parties which rivalled those given by the court-esans in the second Empire which at the time had been the talk of Europe.

There were race-meetings and duels in the Bois.

Everything was headily emotional, especially for a man as attractive as young René.

His father's decision had come like a bombshell.

He accepted it however because it was part of his family tradition that the heir to the Dukedom should marry young and have a number of sons.

He met his future bride only after both families had agreed they were to be married.

He found her, as he expected, young, dull and not particularly attractive.

All that mattered to his father and to her father was that the blood of each was equally blue.

Two of the most ancient families in France would be united as they had once been in the past.

Preparations went ahead for the wedding at which the whole social world would meet.

The honeymoon was conventionally arranged to take place in Venice, which was undoubtedly the most romantic place in Europe.

Two weeks before the marriage was to take place, the bride fell from the bedroom window of her home, 80 feet onto the tiled ground beneath it.

No one knew how it happened.

Whether it was an intentional fall or an accident.

The fact that the girl was dead was a tremendous shock to her parents and to René de Sahran.

His future wife was still almost a stranger to him, and now for the first time he thought of her as perhaps holding strong feelings of her own.

Perhaps she did not wish to marry!

She had, however, not given him any reason to think that was what she felt.

When he looked back he realised he had had little conversation with her.

They had in fact never been alone, since that was considered incorrect at the time.

René told himself that never again would he be put in the ignominious position of being part of an arranged marriage.

"You will get over the shock, dear boy," the old *Duc* said.

"I have no intention father, of marrying anyone," his son had answered.

It was difficult for anyone to believe that was what he really felt.

When he came into the Dukedom, the older members of the family pressed him to produce an heir.

He repeated firmly, in a manner which prevented them from arguing with him, that he had no intention of marrying.

Now Yvonne, who had been his mistress for the last nine months, stared at him as if she could not believe her ears.

"Married?" she exclaimed. "But why, why?"

"For various reasons, which I do not wish to go into," the *Duc* said. "But shall I say the combination of Lord Waterforde's horses and mine will make us invincible on every racecourse in the world."

"But you are not marrying his horses," Yvonne said sharply.

The *Duc* smiled.

"Perhaps I am. And what could be more attractive? Especially when we win every classic race here and in England."

"I cannot understand why you talk in this frivolous manner," Yvonne complained. "We have been so happy! How can you throw all that away just to have a wife? And what is this girl like?"

The *Duc* rose to his feet.

"It is a mistake for us to quarrel," he said. "I want to thank you for the happiness you have given me, and I wish you every happiness in the future."

Yvonne moved off the sofa very swiftly.

Her arms went round the *Duc's* neck and her body, soft and sinuous, pressed against his.

"How can I let you leave me?" she asked, as her lips were against his.

He kissed her.

Then as if a fire was lighted in them both, they moved without speaking from the Drawing-Room into Yvonne's bedroom.

. . . .

It was several hours later when the *Duc*, driving his Chaise, swept up the *Champs Élysèes*.

He was late for an appointment in his house which was near the Bois, and he knew the man he had invited to meet there would expect an explanation.

If he told him the truth, he would not be surprised.

It was what was expected of him.

He thought however that he had perhaps made a mistake.

He had felt for some time that his liaison with Yvonne was not as alluring as it had been at first, and that he should bring it to a close.

The trouble was he became bored with these *affaires* long before the woman with whom he was involved did.

There were invariable tears and innumerable questions of "What have I done? How have I upset you?" and "Why do you no longer love me?"

He had heard them repeated dozens and dozens of times.

The trouble was he had no answer.

Why did a woman become boring, however beautiful she might be?

Why after he had made love to her for two or three months did he suddenly have no wish to see her anymore?

He had often asked himself why it happened, but he could find no convincing explanation.

The women he had chosen who had pursued him as a huntsman pursues a deer, were invariably beautiful, witty and amusing.

It was impossible when he first met them to find fault or to discover a flaw in the perfection of the jewel.

Yet sometimes in a few weeks, usually after two or three months, the end was inevitable.

Time after time as he left a woman weeping, the *Duc* would ask himself what had gone wrong and why he felt as he did.

But he could find no plausible answer.

He knew his contemporaries found it inexplicable that he should wish to leave the most beautiful woman in Paris, or one who was noted for her wit, or who was rich enough to ask him for nothing but himself.

"Why, why, why, does it happen?" the *Duc* had asked the morning sun as he drove home after a last "Goodbye".

He knew now as he drove up the *Champs Élysèes* he had no intention of ever going again to the little house in the *Rue de Rivoli* where he had spent so much time in these past months.

Yvonne was spoken of as quite the most beautiful woman in Paris at the moment.

Her face had made every artist wish to immortalise it on canvas, and her figure had been compared to the finest Greek statues both in Paris and in Rome.

She was witty in that everyone who dined at her table found themselves laughing at the *doubles entendrés* which lay beneath many of the things she said.

"She was also in many ways," the *Duc* thought, "compassionate to those not so fortunate as she was herself."

He hated women who were hard and who pushed themselves into prominence.

If ever Yvonne had done this, she had done it so skilfully that he had not been aware of it.

"The truth is," he told himself as he neared his own house, "I am getting old, too old to spend every night leaving a warm bed at chilly dawn. I intend to settle down in the country with my family and horses."

Then he laughed at himself.

He knew that this was exceedingly improbable.

The next time he saw a lovely unknown face on the horizon, he would inevitably pursue her.

Perhaps the truth was, he enjoyed the chase more than the capture.

There was something exciting in getting to know the unknown, in finding the unexpected when he least expected it.

Then he told himself he had made a decision and would not go back on it.

He had told Lord Waterforde he would marry his daughter, and that was what he intended to do.

Tomorrow he would leave for Provence and be waiting at the Château where she was to join him from the finishing-school where she had been completing her education for the last two years.

She would be young, innocent and unspoilt, and all that she would know about love he was going to teach her.

It was essential that the Duchess of Sahran should be completely pure and never look at any other man but himself.

The *Ducs* down the centuries had all indulged in the amusements of Paris, and had sooner or later enjoyed liaisons with other women besides their wives.

It was however all done with discretion and as much as possible kept from gossiping tongues of those who had nothing better to talk about.

The *Duc* had never at any time contemplated marrying anyone like Yvonne.

At the same time, he thought it would be hard to forget how she had said to him when they were lying in her bed in her fragrant scented room:

"If you want to marry anyone, why do you not marry me, René? I love you and I would make you a very good wife."

The *Duc* had found it hard to believe his ears.

It had never struck him for one instant that Yvonne wanted to marry anyone, even himself.

She had had a number of lovers and had made no secret of it.

But he could not help being aware that what she felt for him was more than just a physical passion.

It was something deeper.

This was in fact an old story, for women invariably fell in love with him and there was nothing he could do about it.

How could he say from the very beginning of an *affaire de coeur*:

"Do not give me your heart because I have no use for it?"

What he wanted was their exquisite bodies, their wit, their companionship, and of course the thrill of fire which he had always found irresistible.

As he thought it over, he could imagine nothing more appalling than being married to Yvonne or her like, and never being certain when he left the house whether another man would be occupying his bed.

"She cannot really have meant it," he told himself as he turned into the gates of his house.

Yet as he drew his horses to a standstill outside the front door, he knew she had meant it, and perhaps was still imagining herself as the *Duchesse* de Sahran.

Waiting for the *Duc* in the equisitely furnished reception room on the ground floor with windows which opened into a large garden, was a man who had been a close friend of the *Duc's* since they first went to school together.

Gustav was a *Vicomte* who had spent as much time as his friend pursuing the beautiful women of Paris.

He was reading the newspaper as the *Duc* entered and as he did so, threw *Le Jour* down on the floor to say:

"You are late, René. I know where you have been, so I will forgive you."

"I am sorry," the *Duc* said. "I have been with Yvonne and have told her my news. When I got there I was carried away."

"I do not blame you," Gustav said. "She is, in my opinion, quite the most beautiful of the women in Paris, and I can assure you that there are a great number of people ready to take your place."

The *Duc* stared at him.

"How do you know I was saying 'Goodbye' to her?" he asked.

"I have known you since we were both ten years old, and I know all the different aspects of your character. One of the nicest things about you is that you are sorry when you have to hurt some woman by saying 'Goodbye'."

"I had no idea I was so transparent," the *Duc* said sharply. "That is in fact what I was doing."

"You told her you were going to get married?" Gustav asked.

"I told her," the *Duc* replied.

"She will be upset," Gustav said reflectively, "for the simple reason that she is fonder of you, I think, than of anyone else. But at the same time, as I have already said, there are plenty of eager young men willing to make up for your absence."

The *Duc* sighed and went to the grog-table to pour Gustav out a small drink.

He was almost totally abstemious because he liked to keep himself perfectly fit for riding.

But at this moment he felt he needed a glass of something to help him forget how Yvonne had wept on his shoulder and suggested that he should marry her.

"What is troubling you?" Gustav enquired.

"Do you want a drink?" the *Duc* asked.

"I have already had one," Gustav replied, "and I would like an answer to my question."

"I can hardly believe it was sincere," the *Duc* said rather reluctantly, "but Yvonne said she would like to marry me."

Gustav looked surprised and then he said:

"Well, that is unusual. I have always believed that the Yvonnes of this world would find it boring to be attached to one man and one man only. But obviously you are the exception to the rule."

"Something I have no wish to be," the *Duc* said, "and I disliked hurting her."

"Of course you did," Gustav replied. "But she will get over it, you can be sure of that."

"I hope you are right," the *Duc* answered. "Now the question is, what shall we do tonight?"

"I have something planned for you," Gustav said. "Fifi is giving a party at her house which I am told will surpass all parties ever given there before, and we are both invited."

The *Duc* laughed.

"I can always rely on you, Gustav," he said. "It will take me out of a depression if I am in one, and find me something to do if I have a moment when I am inactive."

"That is what friends are for," Gustav said. "So we will go to Fifi, and incidentally it will be a cheap evening as everything is being paid for by Von Baret."

"The rich German?" the *Duc* said. "Well he certainly can afford it."

He spoke in such a way that his friend looked at him sharply.

"Are you feeling the pinch, René?" he asked. "Has Yvonne been more extravagant than usual?"

There was a little pause before the *Duc* said:

"If you want the truth, 'Yes', to both those questions."

"So that is why you are marrying Lord Waterforde's daughter," Gustav said. "I rather suspected it, but I cannot believe that you of all people are running short of cash."

"Things have been very difficult this past year," the *Duc* explained. "I have a great many structural repairs to make to the Château, and I was perhaps somewhat extravagant in the pictures I bought for the gallery."

"Château, always the Château," Gustav remarked. "Well, I can understand it, but I always thought you wealthy landowners were never short of a few million Francs."

"I wish that were true," the *Duc* said. "Unless I dismiss some of the people I employ, discontinue the improvements on the estate which I consider essential, and curb my own personal extravagances, I have to have more money."

"Now I understand," Gustav replied. "Which brings us of course to Waterforde's daughter."

"He is very anxious for me to collaborate with him in

forming the finest stable of horses in Europe," the *Duc* said, "and you know that will cost money. I also wish to put this new electric lighting into the Château, which will make all the difference to it."

"Now you are certainly moving with the times," Gustav said. "But I believe the installation of electric lighting is very expensive."

"So is anything if it is properly done," the *Duc* added. "It would make all the difference to those long corridors, and of course would save the expenditure on candles which is astronomic."

Gustav laughed.

"Only because you insist on having the chandeliers lit."

"What is the use of a chandelier unless it is lit?" the *Duc* enquired. "But seriously, though of course I have not told this to anyone else, I am considerably overdrawn at the Bank."

"I think you are very sensible," Gustav said, "in marrying an English girl who will obviously adore you and behave in exactly the way you expect the *Duchesse* de Sahran to behave."

"Of course," the *Duc* said.

"I will doubtless drink your health a thousand times before you put the ring on the bride's finger, so I will not do it now," Gustav went on. "But as my closest friend and as a man I admire tremendously, I wish you, old boy, the very best of luck. Quite genuinely you deserve it."

"Thank you," the *Duc* said.

He drank his own health and as he did so, thought that luck was what he needed, and he needed it more urgently than he had admitted to his friend, Gustav.

As he put down his glass he could hear, almost as if she were in the room, Yvonne saying as he left her:

"I will never forgive you, never, and some day I will make you as unhappy as I am now."

41

Chapter Three

As they drove away from the railway-station into the countryside, Celita found herself thrilled by the beauty of it.

By the Vineyards that were everywhere, the forests of trees, and the distant mountains rising higher and higher.

It was a part of France that she had not known before.

She had, however, read about it and knew a great deal of its history.

She was also aware that Provence to most Frenchmen was the most beautiful part of their country.

Here at least there was something new for her to enjoy.

Yet she knew it was going to be spoilt if Judy was unhappy.

How could Lord Waterforde really be so indifferent to his daughter's feelings?

Surely he must understand that as Judy was so young she wanted time to grow up and make her own life apart from his.

Celita tried to visualise herself saying this to Lord Waterforde, but knew it would be impossible.

He was one of those men who was quite certain that whatever he thought was right.

That what he decided was right for other people, regardless of their own feelings.

If it was to be a battle between him and Judy, she would not have a chance.

It would be one-sided from the word "go".

"What can I do, what *can* I do?" Celita asked herself.

There was one obvious answer which she really dared not put into words.

It was that she should help Judy to run away with Clive Cunningham.

But if she did that, she knew how furious Lord Waterforde would be.

It would put her and her mother in a hopeless position which they could not afford.

The carriages had now left the level plain and were moving up a long steep slope.

Celita could feel the horses straining almost towards the clouds.

A thought suddenly came to her.

It was almost as if it was a message from Heaven.

She grasped at it with two hands and with her heart.

The only possible way she could help Judy was if somehow she could persuade the *Duc* not to propose marriage to her.

There was still a long way to go, but the scenery, the view and the mountains became more beautiful every mile.

Even Judy came out of her despondency to exclaim at the loveliness of the gorges they passed.

They fell down below the road and they could see cascade after cascade splashing over the rocks.

At last the country seemed to be more thickly wooded and there were a number of small villages in the distance.

When they finally turned in through some magnificent gates Celita felt herself holding her breath.

Soon there was the first sight of the Château, and she knew that it might have stepped out of a fairy-story.

It was very large and very impressive.

In front of it there were three large fountains playing, the water glistening iridescent like a thousand rainbows as it caught the sunshine.

"We are here, Dearest," Celita said and then realised that Judy had shut her eyes.

"I do not .. want to .. look," she wailed. "I want to .. go home. Oh! Celita, I want to go . . . back to .. England."

Celita thought hastily that she might have anticipated this and she put her arm around her friend.

"Now listen, Dearest," she said. "I have thought of a way by which I hope I can save you. It is very, very important that you should behave quite normally, otherwise it may make things more difficult than they are already."

"You have thought of a way?" Judy gasped. "What way?"

"There is no time to tell you now," Celita answered, "but please trust me when I say you must act as if you have no idea anything unusual is happening. You have just been invited here as a visitor, because the *Duc* knows your father."

Judy stared at her, and then because she had always let Celita lead her from the time they were children she said:

"I will try to do what you say, but it is going to be difficult."

"Tell yourself that you are acting a part which will help to prevent your having to marry the *Duc*," Celita urged. "If you remember that all the time, it will not be so difficult."

"You are quite certain I shall not have to marry him?" Judy asked.

"We cannot be certain of anything," Celita said. "But if we use our brains and pray very hard for help, I feel sure we shall win."

Judy flung herself against her.

"Oh! Celita, I love you! You have always got me out of trouble and you must save me now! There is no one else who can help me – except you."

Celita knew this was true.

But she was worried in case Judy should make a scene and they would start off on the wrong foot.

"Wipe your eyes, Dear," she said, "and let me tidy your hair."

She pushed aside some of Judy's fair curls and waited until she had wiped her eyes.

Her lashes were still a little wet and therefore darker.

Celita thought it made her even prettier than ever.

"Now, courage!" she admonished. "Remember we are fighting a battle which we have to win."

"We must win, we . . must," Judy said passionately.

As she spoke the carriage came to a standstill outside an extremely impressive front door.

Servants came hurrying down a red carpet.

The girls were helped out and walked up the steps hand in hand.

At the top was a grey-haired magnificent Major-Domo who bowed, welcomed them in French, and asked them to follow him.

Celita, still holding Judy's hand, realised her friend was trembling and thought it was not surprising.

The huge hall was so grand as to be almost awesome.

There were at least six footmen in a very picturesque livery on duty.

The Major-Domo led the way with a flourish across the hall.

He opened the door of a room which was almost as large and exquisitely furnished.

Even at a glance, Celita was aware of the painted ceiling, of the walls decorated in what she knew was the fashion before the Revolution.

On one wall there hung some beautiful tapestries.

It was however difficult to look at anything but the far end of the room.

In front of an enormous marble mantle-piece were standing two men.

As she and Judy walked towards them, one detached himself from the other.

Celita knew this must be the *Duc.*

Her first glance told her that he was taller and even more handsome than she had expected.

His hair was dark and swept back from a square forehead.

His skin was fair and he might almost have been English.

His features were clear cut and his eyes seemed somehow to be twinkling with amusement.

They gave him the raffish look she had expected.

"Welcome," he said, speaking very good English with only

a touch of an accent. "I hope you have had a comfortable journey."

He paused in front of the girls and said:

"Now which of you owns Lord Waterforde and his marvellous horses as a father?"

The way he spoke made even Judy give a little giggle before she said:

"I am Judy Forde," and held out her hand.

"I am delighted to meet you," the *Duc* said. "And this, of course, is Lady Celita."

Celita gave him her hand.

As his fingers closed over it she had the feeling that his vibrations were very strong.

He was in fact far more of a personage than she had expected.

They moved towards the fireplace and were introduced to the *Vicomte*, who Celita thought had a very charming manner.

"Your Aunt, Lady Hilton, has already arrived," the *Duc* said to Judy, "and is upstairs resting after her long journey."

"Oh! she is here!" Judy murmured.

"As I have three English guests," the *Duc* went on, "I have ordered afternoon tea for you which I hope you will appreciate."

"Of course we will," Celita said. "But as we have been at school in Paris we are quite used to not having tea."

"I had forgotten that is where you have been," the *Duc* said. "Did you enjoy your time there?"

Judy had lapsed into silence and Celita found herself doing the talking.

As she did so she was well aware that the *Duc* was sizing them both up, especially Judy.

She saw the sideways glance he gave her after he had asked something to which she did not respond.

She thought with a sinking heart, there was no doubt he intended to marry Judy and it was going to be a very difficult thing to prevent.

To make the conversation easier, Celita said how much she admired the Château and that she had heard how he had tried to restore it to the magnificence it had had before the Revolution.

"My Great-Great-Grandfather spent a fortune on it," the *Duc* said, "and various other members of the family contributed when it was being built and furnished."

"And you have got back many of the things that were stolen?" Celita questioned.

"A great number of them," the *Duc* replied. "Unfortunately I have never been able to discover where the gold plate, which was the finest set in the whole of France, went to. Or the jewels which had been worn by so many of my ancestors and were almost museum pieces."

"I suppose someone, somewhere in the world, is lucky enough to be wearing them," Celita said, "and imagining that she is the *Duchesse* of Sahran."

The *Duc* laughed.

"I doubt if today that would be the height of her ambition. She would wish to be Queen Victoria, or at the very least one of her numerous and distinguished family."

Celita knew he was paying her a compliment and said:

"I think Queen Victoria was delighted to own the French furniture which came from Versailles. It was, as I am sure you know, bid for a auction by the then Prince of Wales's Chef, who was the only person he could think of at the time who spoke French."

The *Duc* laughed.

"I have heard that story, but I do not believe it is true."

"I expect it is," Celita insisted. "After all the English never bother to learn other people's languages. They just shout loudly at the natives, and are furious when they still do not understand."

"I suppose you, Lady Celita, are an exception," the *Duc* said.

"I can speak French," Celita admitted. "I am also quite

fluent in Italian. It is only German that I find a rather ugly language."

"I agree with you," the *Duc* said.

"And of course," Celita went on, "I must congratulate you, Your Grace, on speaking extremely good English."

"That is hardly surprising," the *Duc* said, "considering I went to school in England."

Celita looked surprised.

"I was not aware of that."

"My father insisted I did so for two years. I must admit I enjoyed it, even though I might say I literally had your language kicked into me."

"In other words you were bullied," Celita said.

"Of course," the *Duc* replied. "The English are terrible bullies when they wish to have their own way."

Celita thought he was being deliberately provocative and she answered:

"I have always understood that diplomatically we are brilliant at using persuasion rather than force."

"That I will concede," the *Duc* said. "But at school I was only a rather tiresome little foreigner who was expected to ask if he wanted anything in a language that the other boys understood."

Celita felt that he was making rather a good story out of it.

At the same time she thought it an excellent idea that anyone of such importance should have been educated partly in England.

He could therefore understand the English rather better than if he had never crossed the Channel.

"I will tell you one thing about your country that I found irresistible," the *Duc* said, "and that was your horses."

"Judy and I have already been told how fine yours are," Celita said. "And I hope while we are here we will be allowed to ride."

The *Duc* looked surprised.

"Is that what you would like to do?"

"Of course!" Celita said. "You cannot believe that we

leave Lord Waterforde's horses in the stables and walk on our flat feet."

The *Duc* laughed.

"I remember that he told me that your family lives on his estate. So of course you were able to exercise his horses with your friend, Judy?"

"We rode every morning," Celita said, "and that is something I have missed greatly in France."

"You did not think of riding in the Bois?" the *Duc* asked.

"I certainly thought of it," Celita replied. "My school-mistress, however, considered any competition with the other riders would not be at all *comme il faut* for a school-girl."

The *Duc* understood exactly what she meant and laughed, so did the *Vicomete*.

"I promise you it will be entirely *comme il faut* for you to ride here tomorrow morning," he said. "And, if you do not find my horses as good as Lord Waterforde's, I shall be very piqued."

Judy was still saying very little and it was a relief when the English tea was brought in.

It was not arranged exactly in the way it was in England but the petits fours were certainly delicious.

The *Duc* asked Judy if she would like to pour out the tea.

Celita felt it was an indication of what he expected her to do in the future.

"I think Celita had better do it," Judy said. "She is much better at that sort of thing than I am."

"Now you are being modest," Celita said quickly.

Turning to the *Duc* Celita said:

"What Judy really means is that I am the dog's-body and do all the jobs no one else wants to do."

"Then there is plenty of scope here for you at the Château," the *Duc* said. "At the moment there are thousands of jobs undone, and crying out to be done."

"That will keep you busy," Celita said without thinking. "It should prevent you from going to Paris and being caught up in all its expensive amusements."

She had not meant to say anything which quite obviously referred to the *Duc's* reputation.

She realised she had made a mistake when he looked at her sharply.

He did not say anything however, and walked towards the tea-table.

Celita poured out the tea.

She was conscious that the cups were of Sèvres porcelain and the silver was very elegant.

It was however, she noticed, all present century work.

She assumed that all the earlier silver, which had been made by the finest silversmiths in France, had been lost in the Revolution.

It was as if the *Duc* could read her thoughts when he said:

"When I read all the items in the catalogues, and see some of the pictures that were painted of the Château at that time, I wonder if I shall be fortunate enough to find any of them again."

"It must be for you the search for the Golden Fleece," Celita said. "But I feel sure if you try hard enough, and if you are really determined, you will succeed in your search."

"Do you expect me to believe that?" the *Duc* asked.

Judy who was listening said:

"You really can believe her! If Celita has a feeling something will happen, then it does. Even when I was quite small and something seemed impossible to me, Celita would assure me that I would attain it or it would happen, and she was always right."

"What a reputation!" the *Vicomete* said. "If you are prepared to look into the future, Lady Celita, I would like you to look into mine."

"I am not a fortune-teller," Celita said. "What I sometimes have is a premonition that something will happen, and if it is very necessary and very right, then it does."

"I can ask for nothing better," the *Duc* said. "But I hope while you are here, Lady Celita, you will concentrate on me."

Celita did not answer, she thought she knew what the *Duc* wanted and that she was determined not to give him.

Not if it concerned Judy.

She persuaded the *Duc* into talking about other things belonging to the Château which had been lost in the Revolution.

"I found those Tapestries," he said, "in a lumber-yard. You would hardly believe it, they had been thrown on one side and forgotten. The man in the lumber-yard was quite astonished when I paid him a good sum for them."

"Less than they were worth to you!" the *Vicomte* interposed.

"I am not as stupid as that," the *Duc* said. "But I assure you he was very grateful for what he received. He told me he had often thought, as they looked rather dirty and dingy, that he would put them on a bonfire."

Celita gave a little cry.

"It is ghastly to think that happens to many things that should be preserved for ever. I would like you to show me everything in this wonderful Château, so that I can always remember it when I return to England."

"You will see everything you want to see," the *Duc* promised. "But you must not talk of leaving when you have only just arrived."

He glanced at Judy again as he spoke, and Celita was well aware of the fear that suddenly appeared in her eyes.

To change the conversation she quickly started to talk about the pictures.

The *Duc* promised to show them the picture gallery.

"There are several pictures in the various other rooms," he said, "which I think you will enjoy, from my own collection. My ambition is to bring the collection up-to-date, so that it includes modern artists besides those that were famous in the past."

"You cannot mean those fellows in Montmartre, who are called Impressionists," the *Vicomte* objected. "They daub away in a very strange manner. I cannot make head nor tail of their pictures."

"That may be true of some of them," Celita admitted before the *Duc* could speak. "But we were allowed to visit Montmartre one day while I was at school, and I was most impressed by their use of colour and the fact that they manage to portray in a few strokes what other artists would labour over for hours."

This started a fierce argument over Impressionist paintings.

Celita was championing them and she thought the *Duc* deliberately opposed her because he enjoyed what was actually a duel of words.

As Judy was rather left out of it, Celita broke the conversation and said:

"As we have been travelling for a long time, I think it would be a good idea if Judy and I rested before dinner."

"Of course," the *Duc* answered. "I should have thought of that before. Tonight we have no guests, but tomorrow I shall ask some of my relatives who live nearby and several friends to meet you."

Again as he said the last word he glanced at Judy.

Celita knew, as if he had said it openly, that what he was doing was introducing her to his family, before he announced she was to be his wife.

The *Duc* escorted them to the staircase in the hall, and when they climbed up it the housekeeper in rustling black silk was waiting for them.

She curtsied with dignity, then went ahead to show them into the two rooms they would occupy.

They were, as Celita expected, extremely impressive and really beautiful.

The ceilings were painted, the beds were draped with silk curtains, and the canopies overhead were carved in gilt.

In fact each room was so lovely that Celita felt she could stand looking at them for hours.

The Housekeeper left them, saying she would send Martha, Judy's lady's-maid, to her.

As the door closed, Judy said:

"I do not like him, he frightens me. I should be very, very frightened to be married to someone like that."

Celita knew this was true and said quietly:

"I thought you would feel like that, Dearest, but for tonight at any rate you must be polite, answer him when he speaks to you, and join in the conversation."

"Why should I?" Judy said poutingly. "I do not want to live here in this great overwhelming Château."

She sighed and then continued:

"I want to live with Clive in a nice English house with an English garden. I have nothing in common with the French."

Celita held out her hand.

"Stop!" she urged. "You are working yourself up unnecessarily. The *Duc* has not yet asked you to marry him, and we are going to do what we can to stop him doing so. But if you appear antagonistic, he might appeal to your father to make you do what he wants."

Judy gave a little scream.

"If he does that, Papa will force me up the aisle! You know he will."

"Then you must be clever," Celita advised. "As the *Vicomte* seems a very nice young man, I suggest you concentrate on him, talk to him and seem interested in what he has to say."

She knew this would be difficult, but less difficult for Judy, who was afraid of everything the *Duc* said and quite incapable, Celita knew, of joining in the conversation they had just had about the Impressionists.

"What I must do," Celita said to herself, "is keep him discussing things which are not in any way connected with marriage, and perhaps for the moment he will forget about it and at least not frighten Judy."

She had the feeling that if she was driven too hard Judy might lose control and tell the *Duc* straight out that she did not like him and did not wish to marry him.

"That would be disastrous," Celita thought, "because it

would infuriate Lord Waterforde and make things more difficult than they are already."

"Now listen, Judy, because Martha will be here at any moment," she said, "just forget what your father said about the *Duc* and pretend that we are here to enjoy ourselves with delightful and good-looking young men."

Judy pouted and was just about to say they were neither of those things, when the door opened.

Lady Hilton came in.

She was wearing a Dressing-Gown and her hair was elegantly done.

Her face was powdered and painted in a manner never used by the Countess.

"Dearest girls," she exclaimed in a rather affected way, "how delightful to see you! I am so sorry I was not downstairs when you arrived, but I was absolutely exhausted after that long journey from England."

She moved towards Judy and put her arms around her and kissed her.

"You are a very clever girl," she said. "I am very proud of you! Are you not excited to think that this wonderful, glorious and delightful Château will be yours?"

Judy stiffened, and quickly before she could say anything Celita said:

"It is delightful to see you, Lady Hilton. Neither Judy nor I have any idea why we are here, except to see the *Duc's* horses before we return to England."

Lady Hilton turned towards her with a look of surprise.

"You mean my brother has not told you the good news?" she asked.

"Lord Waterforde," Celita answered, "said we were to meet you here, and he felt sure that both Judy and I would look forward to seeing this famous Château."

Lady Hilton was obviously nonplussed.

She glanced first at Judy, then Celita, as if she thought there must be some mistake.

Then she said:

"Of course that is what he intended. We must not rush our fences, must we?"

"I think that would be a great mistake," Celita said quietly.

Lady Hilton was quick-witted enough to take the hint.

"Yes, yes, of course," she said. "It will be a great advantage to you two, coming straight from school, to see a little of the social life of France before you start the Season in London."

Celita smiled.

"That is what we are both looking forward to," she said, "first the Ball that Lord Waterforde is giving in Park Lane, and most of all the one at Waterforde Court."

"And I am looking forward to that too," Lady Hilton said. "I am having a most spectacular gown made for the occasion."

"Oh, do tell me about it!" Celita said, simulating an interest she was far from feeling.

When finally Lady Hilton left them to rest before they had their baths, Judy said:

"It was clever of you, Celita, to pretend we do not know why Papa has sent us here. Otherwise she would continue to make embarrassing remarks like what she said just now."

"I know that," Celita said. "If I get a chance, I will say to her that you have no idea what your father is planning, and it would be a great mistake to frighten you."

"But I am frightened," Judy said, "so frightened that I wish we could go away tonight and return to England before anyone can stop us."

"That is something we cannot do," Celita said, "so we must be very clever. Please, Judy, do exactly what I tell you. Talk animatedly with the *Vicomte* and be polite if the *Duc* speaks to you."

"I will try," Judy said, "but you know it is not going to be easy."

"What is going to be easy," Celita said, "is riding tomorrow morning. Now there is a subject on which you can really talk without feeling embarrassed and wondering if there is a double entendre behind everything they say to you."

"You mean I can talk about horses?"

"You know a great deal about them," Celita said, "and you have ridden every kind of horse from an ordinary hack to Arab-bred race-horses since you were very small."

She paused and then continued:

"It is something that interests him, so keep to that subject, at least until we see what other obstacles are waiting for us."

She spoke a little anxiously.

Then Judy said:

"But they are there, the obstacles, and the biggest one is when the *Duc* asks me to marry him."

"That is what we have got to prevent him doing," Celita said. "You must help me and do exactly what I tell you."

"I will do anything, anything," Judy said, "rather than marry him and be shut up here in this enormous house, when I might be with Clive."

She gave a big sigh before she said:

"I would be perfectly happy with him in a tiny cottage, and if Aunt Mabel thinks I should be impressed with the *Duc* and what he possesses, then she should marry him herself."

Celita laughed.

"I think even the *Duc* would be afraid of that!"

Suddenly the funny side of it struck Judy too, and she giggled.

Celita kissed her.

"That is better," she said. "Now you look more like yourself. Laugh and try not to be frightened. We are going to win, I am not certain how, but I promise you, Dearest, we are going to win a very difficult battle even though the odds are against us."

Chapter Four

Riding over the level ground at the back of the Château, Celita thought she had never enjoyed anything more.

The horse the *Duc* had chosen for her was very spirited.

At the same time he was easy to handle and went like the wind.

She could say the same of the horse that Judy was riding, and also of the two fine stallions on which the *Duc* and the *Vicomte* were mounted.

She had no idea when she had pressed her horse ahead, that the *Duc* was looking at her with surprise.

He was thinking she was without exception the best woman rider he had ever seen.

Judy was good, but Celita had something about her which was exceptional.

She herself would have said that it was because her Father had taught her to love horses when she was still in the cradle.

He had lifted her up to pat them, and had taught her how to talk to them and how to gain their confidence before she rode them.

The *Duc* was aware that before they set off, Celita had caressed and talked to the horse on which she was now mounted.

He had led the way, and watching him Celita thought that he looked a part of his horse.

It would be impossible for anyone to look more handsome or more at home on that particular stallion.

When they let the horses have their heads, it became a race.

Although Celita surged ahead, she was well aware that the *Duc* could overtake her when he wished to do so.

Only when they pulled in their horses and she turned to smile at the other riders did he say:

"I congratulate both ladies. I can only say that my horses are honoured by their presence."

"That is a very pretty speech," Celita said. "Now I want to know where you have your jumps."

For a moment the *Duc* seemed to hesitate, as if he thought they would be too much for her.

Then he said:

"I will take you to my Private Race Course. I completed it only two years ago. It has been a great success, so I hope you will admire it."

He went ahead through a small wood and there beyond it, was the Race-Course.

Celita knew that it was beautifully laid out.

She appreciated that there were stands for the public and that everything was provided as if they were at Newmarket or Ascot.

"Now I know," she exclaimed, "why your horses win in England."

"I admit that I have copied an English Race-Course," the *Duc* said, "because they are the best I have ever seen."

Celita smiled.

"I know that Lord Waterforde would be delighted to hear you say that."

"He has won so many races in England," the *Duc* said, "that now he is determined to lead the way in Europe. But I think that over here my horses are better than his."

There was a note of satisfaction in the *Duc's* voice which Celita did not miss.

She was sure he was thinking how easy it would be to improve his own horses with Judy's money.

It certainly seemed impossible to think that the *Duc* might be hard up.

This morning, when she was dressing and Martha was helping her, Celita said:

"Is everything as luxurious below stairs as it is above?"

"It is indeed, M'Lady," Martha replied. "but they say *Monsieur's* going through a hard time. I cannot think why: there be no signs of it here."

It was quite obvious that Martha approved of the Château.

Celita thought that here was someone who would be encouraging Judy to marry the *Duc*!

It would make her more depressed than she was already.

Looking at the *Duc* now on a horse which must be worth an enormous sum of money, with hundreds of acres of his own land all round him and his fantastic Château in the distance, it was ridiculous to think that he would be in any way hard-up.

"Then why does he want the money," she asked, "unless it is just greed?"

They went over the jumps, rather carefully at first because they were higher than Celita had expected.

But her horse leapt them with inches to spare and Judy's did the same.

It was then the *Vicomte* suggested that they should have a race adding:

"But of course the Ladies shall have a start."

Everyone thought this was a good idea and as they got into their places the *Vicomte* said mischievously:

"I hope the prize is worth winning."

"Is there one?" Judy asked innocently.

"There will be if I have anything to do with it," the *Vicomte* replied.

For a moment there was silence, then the *Duc* said:

"All right, I have got the message! There will be a prize, and I only hope the best horse wins it."

The two girls were given quite a long start and when the race began Celita thought it would be easy to win.

But she was aware of what a brilliant horseman the *Duc* was.

Although she tried her very hardest to pass the Winning Post first, he beat her by a head.

She knew it was what he deserved, and as they pulled in their horses she said:

"I might have guessed that you would defeat me at the last moment."

"Why do you say that?" he asked.

"It would be a mistake to make you more conceited than you are already," Celita answered provocatively, "so I shall not answer that question."

The *Duc's* eyes were twinkling.

"You are very frank, Lady Celita," he said. "That is something I do not expect in an English Débutante."

"I must try to play my part more in character," Celita said. "And thank you for one of the most exciting races in which I have ever taken part."

The *Vicomte* was saying the same thing to Judy as they rode back towards the Château.

As they were ahead, Celita pulled back her horse so that she and the *Duc* were out of earshot.

With an effort, because she was rather nervous, she said:

"I want to have a private conversation with you, *Monsieur*, when you can spare the time."

The *Duc* raised his eyebrows, but he replied:

"Yes, of course. If you would come to my Study after Breakfast, I shall be signing my letters and we will not be disturbed."

"Thank you."

She rode on quickly, fearing that he might ask her what she wanted to speak to him about.

He made no effort to catch up.

When they left the horses at the Front Door and went into Breakfast he made no reference to what she had said.

Lady Hilton did not appear at Breakfast, which was a relief.

Celita had thought last night it would have been much more enjoyable if she had not been present.

She had tried to impress herself on the *Duc*, and kept

interrupting any more serious conversation with rather stupid remarks.

Breakfast was quite a large meal because at least the men were hungry.

It was in a different room from where they had dined last night.

The walls were panelled and hung with some delightful portraits of the *Duc's* ancestors.

They made Celita remember she had not yet seen the Picture Gallery.

She thought there were so many things to see and do outside the Château that she must be careful not to miss anything inside before she left.

The *Vicomte* was teasing Judy who was laughing.

Celita thought that the house-party was very different to what she had expected and certainly far easier.

She had thought that the French were usually very stiff if they were of any importance.

But there was nothing stiff about the *Duc.*

Especially when he was talking about his horses and other things he wanted to show them in the grounds of the Château.

"I have a private Gorge of my own," he said, "which I think is quite impressive. The Cascade itself is really beautiful. It is a pity, Lady Celita, that you are not an artist! A great number have come here and tried to put it on canvas. In my opinion they have always failed."

"I must see that," Celita said, "and I have heard of the enormous gorges in the Grand Canyon of Provence."

"They are not far from here," the *Duc* said, "so if you stay long enough we will drive over and you shall see what it means to drop a thousand feet from the roadway into the gorge below."

Judy gave a little cry.

"I am sure I should have vertigo," she said. "If it is a question of looking down a thousand feet, I shall be far too frightened to do so."

"I shall not let you fall," the *Vicomte* said gallantly.

Judy smiled at him.

She certainly seemed less depressed than she had been on their arrival.

But Celita knew she was making every effort to avoid being close to the *Duc*.

When he did approach her, even accidentally, there was a touch of fear in her eyes.

"The sooner I talk to him about it the better," Celita told herself as they finished breakfast.

The *Duc* left first saying to the *Vicomte* as he did so:

"Look after our guests, Gustav. I shall be at least an hour with my letters and the people I have to see. When I have finished I will join you in the Music-Room."

Celita had already seen the Music-Room which was at the other end of the Château looking out over the garden.

It was where, she had learnt, the guests often danced.

The walls were exquisitely painted with strange musical instruments while the ceiling was a riot of cupids blowing trumpets and clashing cymbals.

It was hard to think that such beautiful work had survived the Revolution.

The *Duc* admitted it had taken a long time to restore it to its original perfection.

They walked from the Breakfast Room now, not hurrying because there was so many things to look at on the way.

The *Vicomte* pointed out some very fine pictures of horses and also furniture which he told them had been stolen from the Château.

The *Duc* had found it in the attic of one house in an obscure village, and brought it back in triumph.

"It must be fun for him trying to find all the things that once belonged here," Celita said.

"He has enjoyed it," the *Vicomte* replied, "but it is a very costly business, as any people who now possess what belonged to the Château are well aware how much he wants to own it again."

"So we are back to money," Celita thought to herself.

She was quite sure the *Duc* would not give up the idea of marrying Judy easily.

She waited nearly half-an-hour before she slipped away without making any explanation.

She hurried from the Music-Room back down the passage to where the *Duc's* Study was situated.

The door was shut and she opened it tentatively.

She thought that if she heard him speaking to anyone she could go away and come back later.

However there was silence, and as she entered the Study she saw the *Duc* seated at a large and very impressive desk.

He rose as she entered and said:

"I was expecting you to join me, Lady Celita."

He came from behind the desk and walked to the fireplace.

Celita followed him and sat down a little nervously on the sofa.

She was wondering desperately how she should begin, and after a somewhat uncomfortable silence the *Duc* said:

"You wanted to see me? Now I am listening."

"What I have to say to you," Celita said, "may make you angry, and therefore I am frightened."

"Of me?" the *Duc* asked. "I assure you there is no need for that. So just tell me what is worrying you."

Celita looked round the room.

"Since I have been here," she said. "I have realised that everything is perfect, and my Maid tells me that you are known as *Monsieur Parfait.*"

The *Duc* laughed.

"That is true. And needless to say the newspapers have gibed at me a great deal for having acquired such a nickname."

"As it is true, it is certainly nothing to be ashamed of," Celita said. "But I cannot understand why, when you have set out always to have around you everything that is perfect, you are prepared to accept second-best in one matter of the greatest importance."

The *Duc* stared at her.

"I cannot understand what you are saying."

Celita drew in her breath.

"Just before Judy and I left Paris," she said, "she received a letter from her Father saying that, instead of returning to England as he had planned we should do, we were to come here."

"I understood," the *Duc* said, "that Lord Waterforde had arranged this with his daughter, but I did not realise he had left it until the last moment."

"It was a great shock to Judy," Celita said, "because her Father intimated that you might .. while she .. was here .. propose .. to her."

Celita had great difficulty in saying the last words, but she forced them from her lips.

She did not look at the *Duc*.

She was aware however, that he had risen from the chair in which he had sat down beside the sofa.

He was now standing with his back to the mantelpiece.

Without looking at him she was sure he was frowning and she felt vibrations coming from him which were somewhat hostile.

"I am sorry to say this to you," she said quickly, "and please do not be angry with me. But as a perfectionist you must realise that this is not the way any woman would want to receive a proposal of marriage."

"I did not know," the *Duc* said after a moment, "that Lord Waterford would reveal to his daughter what had been a confidential conversation between ourselves, and what my intentions were."

"It was a very great shock to Judy," Celita said, "because we were expecting to return to London for the Season as Débutantes. Then her Father intimated that instead she must .. consider marriage with .. you."

She thought as she finished speaking that this seemed rather a bald statement, but it was difficult to put it in any other words.

Now she glanced up at the *Duc* and saw that he was indeed frowning.

There was silence before he said:

"Are you trying to tell me, Lady Celita, that your friend Judy does not wish to marry me?"

For a moment Celita wondered if she should tell the truth or prevaricate.

Then she said:

"Unknown to Lord Waterforde, Judy is very much in love."

"In love!" the *Duc* exclaimed. "Of course I was not told of this."

"Why should you be?" Celita asked. "Judy is a girl you have never seen and whose one attraction for you is not her beauty nor her personality, but something very different."

Now she feared she was being somewhat offensive.

But it was impossible not to tell the truth.

"You say that Lord Waterforde has no idea that his daughter is in love?" the *Duc* asked.

"None at all. I was doubtful from the beginning if he would allow her to marry Clive Cunningham. There was however just a chance, which of course was swept away when you appeared on the scene."

The *Duc* did not speak and after a moment Celita said:

"How can you as a perfectionist think of marrying, unless it is a case of the perfect love which everyone seeks and a few are fortunate enough to find?"

She spoke in a low voice and now the *Duc* turned his head to look at her.

"What are you talking about?" he asked.

"I am talking about perfect love which you, in particular, should be looking for," Celita answered. "Just as you have made this Château absolutely perfect, just as the grounds are like a dream, surely the woman who becomes your wife must be the other half of yourself."

She paused and as the *Duc* did not speak, she went on:

"She will give you the love which, though you may not be

aware of it, you have been seeking, however much you have enjoyed yourself in . . other directions."

Now the *Duc* was staring at Celita as if he could hardly believe what she was saying.

But she felt as if the words just came to her lips and they flowed out without any effort.

"Are you really saying," the *Duc* asked after a moment, "that you think it is possible for all men, and especially some-one like myself, to find the love which is written about by poets and painted in some of the pictures in my Gallery?"

"But of course I do," Celita replied, "and that is what you should be looking for, not making an arranged marriage."

"I did not intend to make an arranged marriage," the *Duc* interrupted angrily. "That is something I have always abom-inated, after what happened to me."

Celita stared at him.

"How can you call it anything but arranged if you told Lord Waterforde that you would marry his daughter because she is so rich, and because she is so rich, Lord Waterforde wants at least a Prince or a Duke as a son-in-law."

"Now just listen to me a moment, Lady Celita," the *Duc* said, sitting down in the chair he had vacated. "I like Lord Waterforde and he is very anxious that we should unite our stables in our attempt to win the French Classic Races. He told me that his daughter was a very idealistic girl who had heard of me and thought of me as a Knight in Shining Armour, living in a Fairy Tale Palace in the most beautiful part of Provence."

Celita gave an audible gasp, but the *Duc* went on:

"When I suggested that I would meet her here, he said that everything could be arranged and it would be for her a dream come true."

Celita was silent for a moment.

She could understand how Lord Waterforde was deter-mined that his beloved daughter would have the very best.

He had appealed to the *Duc* in a manner which he knew was almost unique.

Of course Lord Waterforde knew the *Duc* was an idealist in his endless search to bring perfection back to the Château in which he had been born.

It should have been for him the beginning of a Fairy Tale that came true.

But it was impossible for the simple reason that Judy was already in love, although her father had no idea of it.

The *Duc* was waiting and after a moment Celita said:

"I am .. sorry! I am .. terribly .. sorry! Everyone has dreams of what they want, which is just out of reach, and Lord Waterforde's dream is that Judy should marry someone of great importance."

"And is that something that she does not want?" the *Duc* enquired.

"All she wants is to live in a nice little English house with a charming, handsome young man, who rides brilliantly, but has not a great deal else to recommend him, except that he loves her with all his heart."

The way that Celita spoke was actually rather moving.

The *Duc's* eyes softened before he said:

"And you are telling me that I must try not to spoil her dream of happiness?"

"What I was really intending," Celita said, "was to ask you for help. I told you the truth about Judy, but Lord Waterforde is a very masterful and very positive man, and when he wants something he expects to get it."

The *Duc* stared at her before he said slowly:

"What you are now saying is that he would be extremely angry both with his daughter and with me, if what he has arranged does not come off!"

"Very angry indeed," Celita agreed, "and I have been trying desperately, ever since we had his letter in Paris, to think of what we could do. First to prevent you from proposing to Judy, and then not to lose Lord Waterforde's friendship because he will be so angry you have not done so."

"I can see that is certainly a problem," the *Duc* remarked.

"I can hear how much this means to you, so forgive me if I ask you how you are involved in this."

Celita thought it was clever of him to realise that she was.

She made a helpless little gesture with her hands as she said:

"My Father was far from being a rich man, and it was Lord Waterforde who suggested that we should give up the huge house which has been lived in by all the Earls of Langdale, and move into a delightful, much smaller Elizabethan house on his Estate."

She paused and then continued:

"After my Father died and my mother was left with very little money, Lord Waterforde has been kindness itself to us. But if he learns I have interfered with one of his most precious plans, he will, I think, be very, very angry with me."

Her voice died away, and she looked at the *Duc* pleadingly, hoping that he would understand.

"I can see, Lady Celita," he said after a moment, "that this puzzle is far more complicated than I thought it to be at first."

He arose from his chair and walked across the room.

"I will be frank with you," he said after a moment, "and admit that I have no wish to quarrel with Lord Waterforde."

"I have heard," Celita said, "that you are hard-up. I cannot believe that is possible."

"It does sound rather absurd," the *Duc* said. "but in fact, in restoring the Château to its former glory I have spent a great deal of money. And things have been rather difficult in France, as you will know, since the Franco-Prussian War."

Celita nodded.

"As head of the Sahran Family, I am responsible for an enormous number of relatives, from Great-Grandparents down to newly born babies, and the truth is I have not enough money at the moment to spend on my horses, which of course are what attracted Lord Waterforde in the first place."

"So you need him as a partner," Celita summed it all up. "As he is a very kind man, it is something you will never regret."

"But how," the *Duc* asked, "are we to avoid, you and I, Lady Celita, upsetting him?"

"I do not know. That is what is worrying me," Celita said. "If he thinks you do not think that Judy is attractive enough, he will feel insulted, and she dare not as yet tell him that she is in love with Clive Cunningham. He comes from an old and distinguished family, and his father is a Baronet, but cannot compare in any way with the *Duc* de Sahran."

The *Duc* made a little murmur before he said:

"You must tell me, Lady Celita, what I can do."

"If I knew I would tell you," she said. "Thank you for not being more angry than you are. I was very, very nervous when I . . came in . . here."

"I am thinking very seriously of what you have said," the *Duc* answered. "I shall now be seeking real love, the Golden Fleece, rather than accepting second best."

"Of course you must do that," Celita said. "One day you will find somebody who is as perfect as your Château, as beautiful as your pictures and who, as she moved about it, you will know was made by God for you."

"How can I be sure that will happen?" the *Duc* asked.

"I feel that that will happen. I really do," Celita said. "You have gone too far now to turn back. There may be a mountain ahead of you to climb, and beyond that another mountain, but in the end you will find what will complete the perfection of '*Monsieur Parfait*'."

The *Duc* laughed.

"Now you are turning it into a Fairy Story."

"It is!" she replied. "It is a Fairy Story! Who could play a part in one better than yourself?"

The *Duc* did not answer.

Then after what seemed a long pause he said:

"Unless we are to make Lord Waterforde the villain of the story, we have to think of a way out."

"I have been thinking and praying," Celita replied.

"I thought you might have been doing that," the *Duc* said. "My Chapel is always open."

"I had forgotten that you must have one," Celita answered. "I will go there to pray very, very hard that you will find an answer to this terrible problem."

The *Duc* walked to the window and looked out.

The fountains were throwing their water into the sky, glinting in the sun as it fell.

It was, he thought, a genuine perfection in a perfect setting.

Then suddenly an idea came to him and he turned round.

"I have thought of something rather clever."

"What is it?" Celita enquired eagerly.

"I shall tell Lord Waterforde when he arrives," the *Duc* said slowly, as if he was thinking of each word before he spoke it, "that the moment I saw you I fell in love with you."

Celita gasped.

"You . . cannot say . . that!"

"Why not? It is something that Lord Waterforde is bound to accept. After all, you came here as part of his arrangement, and from what you have said, I am sure that he is very fond of you. We can say there is no hurry for us to marry, or even to announce our engagement, because you wish to do the Season with Judy."

"That is true!" Celita murmured.

"By the time that is over Lord Waterforde will be my partner," the *Duc* continued, "and if, which of course is very likely, you find someone you love or feel you do not wish to marry a Frenchman, we can terminate our association, which anyway has been secret, with no hard feelings from anyone."

While he was talking, Celita was looking at him with wide eyes.

At first she thought that the whole idea was impossible, ridiculous, absurd!

Then as the *Duc* finished speaking she saw how clever it was.

Lord Waterforde *was* very fond of her.

He would certainly not wish to upset her Mother by quarrelling over the fact that she was engaged to the man he had wanted as his own son-in-law.

As the *Duc* had said, by the end of the Season, their racing partnership would be tied up neatly.

He and Lord Waterforde would be running their horses together.

She could then say that she had no wish to marry the *Duc* and they could part on friendly terms.

Celita clasped her hands together.

"All . . right," she said. "It is . . brilliant of . . you to . . think of such . . a plan! Are you quite . . sure that . . you do not . . mind pretending . . . to Lord Waterforde that . . you are . . in love with me . . ?"

There was a twisted smile on the *Duc's* lips as he said:

"I hope I am a good enough actor for the part."

Celita gave a little laugh.

"From all accounts you have had a great deal of experience."

"Now you are being impertinent," the *Duc* protested. "It is something I shall definitely not tolerate in my fiancée."

Then they were both laughing.

Laughing because the tension was over.

Just for the moment it all seemed very funny.

When they went back to join the others, Celita could not help feeling as if she had passed through a very emotional experience.

It had been nerve-racking, yet in a miraculous way she had survived.

Judy had guessed that she had gone to talk to the *Duc*.

As Celita re-joined her and the *Vicomte* in the Music Room, there was a questioning expression in her eyes.

Celita smiled at her and a few minutes later took her hand and squeezed it.

"It is all . . right," she said in a whisper.

"You are certain?" Judy enquired.

Celita nodded.

The *Duc* had been talking to the *Vicomte* and now he said:

"We are wasting this very fine morning. What would you like to do?"

"I would like to ride again after tea when it is cooler," the *Vicomte* said, "and now, why do we not walk down to the Cascade? I have been telling Judy about it, and she is very interested."

Celita noticed that he was calling Judy by her Christian name and thought that it was a step in the right direction.

Anything that prevented Judy from being tense and worried was in itself a blessing.

They went out of the French windows at the end of the Music Room and into the garden.

It was hot, but not too hot for the walk across the green lawns.

Beyond them lay the formal gardens which the *Duc* said covered one hundred and fifty acres.

They were the finest example of highly stylized French landscaping in the world.

To Celita they were enchanting in the way they were laid out.

Besides the fountain there was a small sculptured pool and clipped yew hedges.

Then beyond them they came to the Cascade.

The *Duc* explained that the water came from the hills which ran through the upper part of his estate.

The stream started high up in the mountains which they could see in the distance.

It flowed down until eventually it fed into a small lake.

From this it fell in the form of a gleaming cascade into a great basin, surrounded by marble statues of Gods and Goddesses.

Finally it fell hundreds of feet into the gorge where the water splashed and tumbled over the rocks until it disappeared into the distance.

It was so unusual and at the same time so attractive that the girls stood looking at it spellbound.

Celita turned to the *Duc* and said in a voice only he could hear:

"Another perfection by '*Monsieur Parfait*'."

The *Duc* smiled.

"I am delighted to accept your praise. But I must confess it was here exactly like this when I was born. The only things I have had to replace were some of the Gods and Goddesses."

"Your statues are beautiful," Celita said.

"They came from Greece," the *Duc* said. "I think you might almost find yourself among them."

"That is a delightful compliment which only a Frenchman could make," Celita teased.

"I am having to polish up my behaviour, my outlook and especially my ambitions," the *Duc* answered. "I can only hope you will not be disappointed with the result."

"It would be very sad if I were," Celita said. "Let me tell you I am not apprehensive. I think '*Monsieur Parfait*', although it is very bad for him, you will always get what he wants."

"I wonder if you are right," the *Duc* said.

Now she thought there was almost a wistful look in his eyes.

They walked about in the garden for some time and then moved back to the house.

As they did so they could see two men at the garden door.

Celita glanced at them and then was aware that a servant in Livery was pointing them out to the man beside him.

She knew as she looked at them again that the visitor was someone she was expecting, but not so soon.

If she had seen Clive Cunningham, so had Judy.

As she stared at him advancing towards them, Celita saw her face was transformed.

It was obviously the expression of a woman in love.

One who was thrilled with what was happening, and was very, very happy.

Celita could only hope that the men would not notice.

Yet she was certain that the *Duc* had, when he stepped forward and holding out his hand said:

"I think you must be Mr. Clive Cunningham. Lady Celita has told me about you."

"I hope I am not intruding," Clive said. "I was very anxious to see Lady Celita, and I was in the neighbourhood."

"Of course we are delighted to welcome you," the *Duc* said, "and I am told you are extremely interested in horses."

"I am indeed," Clive answered.

He went towards Celita first and she said:

"How lovely to see you, Clive."

Then he turned towards Judy.

Celita knew it was with the greatest difficulty that she did not throw herself into his arms.

Then as he took her hand, her fingers clung to his.

Only someone quite blind would not have realised that the rather dull, apathetic young woman, who had not taken much interest in anything, had suddenly woken up.

"We have been looking at the Cascade," Judy said. "You must see it, you really must!"

"I am sure it is magnificent," Clive replied.

"Then come and look at it now, while we are here," Judy begged.

Celita felt there was nothing she could do, and the *Duc*, who was well aware of the situation, said:

"That is a good idea. You show Mr. Cunningham the Cascade and then join us in the Music Room. I want to show Lady Celita some pictures of the Cascade and a plan of the gardens."

Judy and Clive were hardly waiting for him to finish before they moved away.

As the three of them walked on towards the Château, Gustav said:

"Surely this is rather a surprise. Who is Clive Cunningham?"

"He lives near us in the country," Celita said quickly, "and he is an outstanding horseman. He wins every Point-to-Point, much to the annoyance of Lord Waterforde."

The two men laughed.

"I can see that must be irritating when you own as many horses as His Lordship does."

"Clive's father is the 5th Baronet and has an attractive but much smaller Estate adjoining Lord Waterforde's."

"I am only surprised," the *Vicomte* said, "that Lord Waterforde has not gobbled it up – the age-old story of the rich Ogre."

"I think Sir Reginald would rather die than sell his house or the Estate," Celita said. "But like everyone else he finds things very expensive today, especially horses."

She could not help glancing at the *Duc* as she spoke.

"That is true enough," the *Duc* said. "You must take Mr. Cunningham round the Race-Course, and he can show us how to win an English Point-to-Point."

Celita looked at him, and as if she had asked the question he said:

'Of course he must stay if he has come so far to see *you*."

He accentuated the last word and she smiled at him.

"That is very kind of you," she said, "and I am sure he will be very eager to do so."

He went into the house and Celita went upstairs to tidy herself before luncheon.

When she had gone the *Vicomte* turned to the *Duc* and said:

"What is going on? I thought you were concentrating on Waterforde's daughter?"

"She is in love with the young man who had just arrived," the *Duc* said bluntly, "but her father has no idea of it."

The *Vicomte* held up his hands.

"More problems! For Goodness sake, René, walk carefully, or you may put your foot in it. You want that money as I well know, if you are to go on living as you are at the moment."

"I think with a little luck we can arrange everything," the *Duc* said, "so pretend to notice nothing and be careful in front of Lady Hilton. It is the gossip-talkers who always ruin everything if they are given a chance."

"That is true enough," the *Vicomte* agreed. "At the same time I admit I am finding myself very much out of my depth. I thought everything was arranged nice and tidily although

I did not exactly approve for you to marry a docile little English girl."

"Now stop pointing and probing," the *Duc* said. "for the moment my attentions are for Lady Celita."

"Now there you have something!" the *Vicomte* asserted. "I find her enchanting, very amusing, and not in the least what I expected in a Débutante who is usually as dull as ditch-water and has no conversation."

"You certainly cannot say that of Lady Celita," the *Duc* observed.

"Personally, I think she is lovely," the *Vicomte* said, "and if you are not claiming priority rights, I might try for a chance myself."

"This is a game, Gustav," the *Duc* said, "in which you are not entered for the prize nor are you allowed to interfere."

"Then what am I to do?" the *Vicomte* enquired.

"Make yourself pleasant on the touch-line, and for Heaven's sake do not make a mess of it."

"What I am asking, is what I am to make a mess of?" the *Vicomte* said plaintively.

Before the *Duc* could answer the door opened and Lady Hamilton came in.

She was dressed with great elegance and her face was made up as if for the stage.

"Oh, here you two boys are!" she said coyly. "I have been feeling rather neglected as I did want to walk in the garden with you."

"I am so sorry," the *Duc* said, "but we felt as we were going down to the Cascade you would find it rather hot and tiring."

"I should indeed, if that is where you have been," Lady Hilton said. "I have just been told that Mr. Cunningham is here. He lives in Berkshire, so why has he turned up?"

"He is travelling in France, so he called in to see his English neighbours," the *Duc* answered, "and as he is very interested in horses, I think I should ask him to stay."

"Horses! Always horses!" Lady Hilton said, holding her hands up.

As she spoke the *Duc* remembered Yvonne saying exactly the same thing.

It struck him that while he had been entertaining his English guests he had actually not given a thought to Yvonne.

It was a relief because he disliked scenes more than anything else.

He had feared that the way she had behaved would worry him, and that he would be wondering if he could have been more tactful and perhaps more gentle with her.

At the same time, he was confident she would soon get over her obsession for him.

A great number of other men would be waiting to take his place.

Then, though he had tried to forget it, he found himself remembering how, when they had been in bed together, she had said in a very soft tone:

"If you want to marry anyone, why do you not marry me, René? I love you and I would make you a good wife."

This had taken him by surprise.

It had never occurred to him for one moment that their association was anything more than an *affaire de coeur.*

Inevitably, like many others in which he had indulged, it would come to an end.

It had been impossible to explain to her that he wanted someone younger and unspoilt, pure and untouched, who would be the mother of his children.

After what Lord Waterforde had told him, the *Duc* had assumed that his young wife would adore him.

He would teach her gently the arts of love, and she would be happy at the Châeau with their children.

But now, after what Celita had told him, he found himself thinking that he had been very foolish and over-optimistic.

He had seen the expression on Judy's face when she saw Clive Cunningham approaching.

It had transformed her completely from a depressed-looking young girl into a woman pulsating with life and the throbs of her heart.

The *Duc* had known in that moment that Celita was right. That was what he should be seeking and that, unless his luck deserted him, was what he was now determined to find.

Chapter Five

Coming in together from riding they went chattering into the Breakfast Room.

It was the fourth day that they had ridden over the flat land and raced each other over the Race-Course.

Celita felt that every time they did so it was more enjoyable than the time before.

"You rode '*Petit Point*' very well today," Clive said to Judy. "I can see he is improving every time you take him over the jumps."

"I do try," Judy said.

She looked up at Clive with an expression of love in her eyes which Celita thought was very touching.

At the same time they had been finding it difficult to conceal from Lady Hamilton what was going on.

It would be a great mistake, Celita had warned Judy and Clive, if she realised it and wrote to report it to Lord Waterforde.

"Yes of course! Papa would be furious!" Judy exclaimed with a little cry of horror.

"We will be very careful," Clive promised.

At the same time it was impossible, because they were in love with each other, not to reveal it.

Every time they spoke or were close together their feelings seemed to vibrate one to the other.

Fortunately, Lady Hilton was so taken up with herself that she did not pay a great deal of attention to other people.

But as the days passed, Celita could not help thinking that

she must be blind, deaf and dumb if she did not realise how happy Judy was and how radiant she looked.

"What are we going to do this afternoon?" Celita asked as she sat down at the table.

"I am waiting to ask our host," Clive replied. "I am sure he has some exciting plan up his sleeve."

The *Duc* enjoyed springing surprises on them.

Last night there had been a huge dinner-party, with more guests coming in afterwards.

They had danced to an extremely good band in the Music Room.

The *Duc* had not said a word until they were going up to dress for dinner, when he had remarked:

"Put on your best clothes, and your most comfortable shoes because you will need them."

Celita stopped on the stairs.

"Are you saying in a roundabout way that we are going to dance?"

"We are," the *Duc* replied. "And I shall be interested to learn if you are as light as you look or as heavy as a sack of potatoes."

"I am not going to rise to that remark," Celita said, "but I shall do my best to stand on your toes if they get in my way."

The *Duc* laughed.

She thought how different he had become in the last few days since their arrival.

Then he had been extremely awe-inspiring.

Now he enjoyed teasing her and being so provocative in his remarks that automatically she answered him back.

"You may be very clever," Judy said to the *Duc*, "but you will never get the better of Celita. She always wins in an argument."

"I refuse to accept that from a mere woman," the *Duc* said.

Celita flung a silk cushion at him, then thought for a moment that perhaps he would be offended.

Instead he threw one back, and was, as he pointed out, a better shot than she was.

It was all great fun and they always seemed to be laughing.

Only in bed last night, after they had danced until one o'clock in the morning, did Celita wonder about the *Duc*.

Did he miss the more exotic and certainly the more unusual amusements of Paris?

Now as he came into the Breakfast Room she thought how handsome he looked in his riding-clothes and at the same time so healthy.

His skin was slightly sun-burnt, his body slim and athletic.

She also thought no man could look more alert.

The *Duc* walked to the top of the table and said:

"I have something to tell you."

They all turned their faces towards him and he said slowly:

"I have received news that your Father, Judy, will be joining us this afternoon."

Celita stiffened.

Judy gave a little cry which was unmistakably one of horror.

"He .. he .. he is .. coming .. here?" she asked, as if she might not have heard aright.

"He will be arriving about two o'clock," the *Duc* said, "and I have arranged for him to have luncheon in the town. That means he should be here at the Château about three."

Judy was hardly listening.

She was holding on to Clive's hand and looking up at him pleadingly.

The *Duc* sat down in his chair as he went on:

"I think you will all agree it would be a great mistake for Lord Waterforde's sister, Lady Hilton, to see him before we do! I have therefore arranged that she will go over to luncheon with a friend who has a very beautiful garden she is anxious to see."

Celita gave a little sigh of relief.

"That is clever you," she said. "Of course we must speak to him first."

"That is what I thought," the *Duc* said, "and I have a suggestion to make of which I think, Judy, you will approve."

"What is that?" Judy asked in a low and depressed voice.

"When I was with your Father at Newmarket, we were told a well-known Peer had died and his stables were to be sold."

Judy was listening, but Celita knew she was wondering how this could affect her.

"Your Father and I went to look at the horses, which we both liked. I was also impressed with the house which was a perfect example of Queen Anne style and in very good repair. It stood in a delightful garden surrounded by fifty acres of land."

He paused and now Celita was wondering why he was telling them all this.

"I have just learnt," the *Duc* went on, "That the bid I made for the whole place has been accepted, and I thought if I offered it to Clive as Manager of my Race-Horses in England it might make his position more important than it is at the moment."

His three guests at the table looked at him with wide eyes and there was dead silence.

Then Judy jumped up from her chair, and running to the top of the table put her arms around the *Duc's* neck.

"You are the .. kindest and most generous .. man in .. the world," she said and kissed his cheek.

As she did so, it suddenly struck Celita that she too had an urge to kiss the *Duc*.

'How can any man think of anything so clever at this difficult moment,' she wondered, 'and at the same time be so understanding about what Judy and Clive are feeling?'

As the *Duc* smiled at Judy, she added to herself:

'He is wonderful! If anyone can make the situation have a happy ending, it will be he.'

The *Duc's* eyes met hers across the table.

She knew he was telling her that he had understood what Judy and Clive felt for each other and believed, as she did, that they had found perfection.

They were however a little subdued as they finished breakfast.

Then the *Duc* said:

"What do you want to do this morning, Clive?"

"I have promised your Chief groom," Clive answered, "that I would take two horses over the jumps which he thinks need a little encouragement. The Bay is certainly rather nervous, but I am sure I can cure her if I have enough time to do so."

"Can I come with you?" Judy asked.

"But of course," he answered.

Celita saw Judy's hand go out to touch his.

"I have to call on a Farmer at the far end of the Estate," the *Duc* announced, "and I thought, Celita, you would come with me."

"I would love to," she answered. "Are we riding or driving?"

"I thought we would drive for a change," he said. "I have a pair of white horses which you have not yet seen, but which I guarantee will break any record that exists so far."

"I shall enjoy that," Celita replied.

Then she went up to change.

She had the frightening feeling that perhaps this would be the last time she would be driving alone with the *Duc*.

If Lord Waterforde was really angry with her, he might send her home in disgrace.

Then her mother would be depressed and anything might happen.

She chose a thin frock as the sun was hot, and an attractive hat which would shade her face without being blown away too easily.

She did not take long.

When she hurried downstairs, it was to find that Judy and Clive had already left for the stables.

The *Duc* was waiting for her in the Hall.

They looked first at the pair of white horses which were certainly outstanding and so alike it would be impossible to tell them apart.

"How could you find anything so unusual?" she asked.

"I bred them," the *Duc* answered.

This was another activity in which Lord Waterforde was interested.

Even to think of His Lordship made Celita give a little shudder.

She had been living in 'Cloud-Cuckoo-Land', she told herself, as she climbed into the Chaise.

Now they had to come back to reality!

As they drove down the drive the *Duc* said:

"Stop being frightened! I have a feeling in my bones that everything is going to be all right."

"I wish I could say the same," Celita answered. "But you know as well as I do he is not going to be pleased that a *Duc* has eluded him, and his daughter will never be more than the Hon. Mrs. Cunningham, however important her husband becomes in the Racing World."

Before the *Duc* could reply she added impulsively:

"It was so kind of you! So very, very kind of you to give Clive that position at Newmarket! It is something he will greatly enjoy and will, I am sure, do extremely well."

"That is what I thought myself," the *Duc* said. "Incidentally, he is a charming young man, and both Gustav and I like him very much."

The *Vicomte* was not with them today because he had to leave very early to visit one of his relatives who lived about twenty miles away.

He had, however, assured them last night that he would be back in time for dinner.

"I am frightened," Celita went on, "that Lord Waterforde will be so disappointed that he will take Judy and me away immediately in disgrace. What will you do then?"

"I shall have to tighten my belt," the *Duc* said, "and decide how I can save the money I need in some way that I have not thought of before. It will be something I shall dislike doing, but it will have to be done."

Celita clasped her hands together.

"I shall be praying. Praying very hard that Lord Waterforde will still want you as his partner even if you will not be his son-in-law. Then at least you can have your horses, your breeding mares, and . . ."

She paused for a moment.

Then feeling that she was being rather dramatic, she said mischievously:

". . . and of course the Perfect Wife, who will not only be exactly as you want her to be, but also extremely rich."

"Now you are asking for too much," the *Duc* said, "and I do not believe the gods expect one to be greedy."

"You want the best," Celita said. "Or, as you yourself would say, perfection."

"And if it eludes me?" the *Duc* enquired.

"Then you will just have to go on looking and looking until you are so old you will be able to hobble no further. You will die thinking the woman of your heart is waiting for you in Heaven."

The *Duc* laughed.

"Judy is right. You have an answer to everything, Celita. But I am rather depressed at the thought of the long years in which I must seek, only to be disappointed."

'Perhaps you will be fortunate enough to find what you want when you least expect it," Celita said. "You must, of course, believe that ultimately you will be the winner."

The *Duc* did not reply but kept his eyes on the road ahead.

She had the feeling, however, that he was thinking over what she had said.

Considering how she and Judy had upset all his plans, he was being very sporting about it.

He was behaving exactly as they might have expected if he had not at first seemed so frightened.

When they reached the farm, which was a very attractive one, the Farmer came out to greet them.

He was delighted that the *Duc* was visiting them.

He informed them that his wife had given birth two days before to their first child.

"Is it a boy or a girl?" the *Duc* asked.

"A boy! *Monsieur le Duc*. We thought, if you do not think it an impertinence, we'd give him your name."

"I should be delighted," the *Duc* said. "Of course I must be his God-Father and give him his first golden Louis so he can start saving."

The Farmer was overcome with delight.

Celita asked if she could see the baby.

He took her into his wife's room and Celita found that she was quite a young woman.

They had been married nearly two years before their first child had arrived.

She was nursing the baby in bed.

She handed him proudly to Celita who saw he was an attractive little boy.

He looked rather like one of the Cherubs painted on the ceilings of the Chapel and he already had a few little curls of dark hair.

Celita took him into her arms and said:

"*Monsieur le Duc* has promised to be God-Father to little René. If you would permit me, I would like to show him the baby."

"Yes, of course," the Farmer's wife said eagerly.

Celita walked out of the bed-room.

She found the *Duc* and the Farmer having a glass of home-brewed cider in the parlour.

"I have brought you your new God-Son," Celita said.

She lifted the baby up in her arms and looked down at him as she did so.

She thought that one day she would want to hold her own son in the same way.

Then perhaps she, like the *Duc*, would have found perfection and they would each be married to the person who was the other half of themselves.

She had no idea how expressive her eyes were as she looked down at the baby.

Then the *Duc*, who had been standing beside her without speaking, said very quietly:

"We shall both find what we seek, if we seek long enough."

Celita looked up at him and smiled.

"You are reading my thoughts, again," she protested. "But you must say he is a very attractive baby."

"Now you are making me determined," the *Duc* said, "to have a large family."

'Of course you must," Celita answered. "Think what a wonderful place the Château will be for them to play in. They will all ride your horses, and find the garden and the fountains an enchantment from the time they are born."

She spoke in a rapt little voice.

The *Duc* did not speak but just stood looking at her.

Then the Farmer, who had gone to get some accounts to show the *Duc*, came into the room and the spell was broken.

Celita took the baby back to his Mother, and soon they were driving away from the farm.

The *Duc* had ordered luncheon to be late, and did not take Celita back the way that they had come.

Instead he diverted their route to include the Grand Canyon of Provence, which Celita had mentioned to the *Duc*.

They drove off the main road and started to climb higher and higher up the side of what seemed to be an enormous mountain.

Celita could hardly believe that the gorges below them were real.

Further on there was a huge drop, as the *Duc* had said, of a thousand feet.

It fell straight down from the road they were on to the narrow winding gorges below with their cascades breaking over the rocks.

But still they went higher and higher until Celita said:

"I am too frightened to look. Suppose you tip us over the edge?"

The *Duc* laughed.

"If I drove as badly as that I would not have risked your life by coming here. I promise you, you are quite safe. You must see how beautiful each gorge is, and of course they all have legends in which the local folk firmly believe."

They twisted and turned for miles.

Then as they began to descend, Celita could not help giving a sigh of relief that they were still unhurt.

When finally they reached the Château, they found Clive and Judy were waiting for them.

"I thought you must be lost!" Judy exclaimed when they appeared.

"We have been looking at the gorges," Celita said, "and you were quite right, Judy, they were terrifying, but very, very beautiful!"

"We have had a wonderful time with the horses," Judy said in an exciting voice. "Clive was so, so clever with them."

She was looking at him with adoring eyes as they went into luncheon.

Although the meal was delicious, Celita felt so nervous that she found it hard to enjoy the specialities the Chef had provided.

When they left the Dining-Room they walked to the Drawing-Room where they were to receive Lord Waterforde.

In silence they each were wondering apprehensively what would happen next.

When the carriage brought Lord Waterforde to the front door, the *Duc* went to meet him.

As he did so Clive said to Judy, as if he had thought of it for the first time:

"Your Father will not be expecting to find me here. Shall I disappear and come back later?"

"You cannot .. leave .. me," Judy cried. "Oh .. Clive .. I am so .. frightened."

"I know, my darling!" he answered. "But you must be brave and pray that your Father will not be as angry as we anticipate."

Celita could not help being sure that he would be very angry indeed.

He would certainly not welcome the news that she would be taking Judy's place as a *Duchesse* de Sahran.

Then they heard Lord Waterforde's voice in the hall talking to the *Duc*.

He came into the room looking very large and over-powering.

Judy ran to greet him.

"It is lovely to see you, Papa," she said in a voice that shook a little. "Did you have a good journey?"

"Very good," he replied.

He kissed his daughter and then kissed Celita's cheek.

"Your Mother sent you her best love," he said.

"Is she well?" Celita asked.

"Very well!' he replied.

Then he looked across the room at Clive and exclaimed in surprise:

"Cunningham! So you are here! I heard you were away, but I did not expect to meet you in France."

"Clive Cunningham is going to be in charge of my horses at Newmarket," the *Duc* said. "You will remember, my Lord, when we were both there I left a bid for Grosvenor Lodge which we both thought an extremely attractive mansion with excellent stables?"

"Yes, of course! Of course!" Lord Waterforde said. "I do remember."

"I have just heard that the bid I put in has just been been accepted, and as Cunningham is so experienced with horses, I can imagine no one better qualified to look after mine when I am not able to be present."

Celita could see that Lord Waterforde was rather surprised by this.

Then, as if he felt this was not of particularly urgent importance, he said to the *Duc*:

"I have something to say to my daughter and to Celita. I wonder if you would permit me to be with them alone for a short while?"

Celita glanced at Judy, and as their eyes met they were both exceedingly apprehensive about what this meant:

"But of course," the *Duc* was saying. "Cunningham and I will go to my Study, and when you join us there are quite a number of things I want to show you. Most important, as you can imagine, are the stables!"

"Yes! Yes!" Lord Waterforde agreed.

The *Duc* and Clive left the Drawing-Room, shutting the door behind them.

Judy sat down on the sofa beside Celita.

Because she was frightened, she slipped her hand into hers and Celita pressed her fingers to reassure her.

Lord Waterforde stood in front of the fireplace and for a moment there was complete silence.

It flashed through Celita's mind that he already knew what had happened.

Perhaps in spite of all their caution Lady Hilton had told him.

After what seemed a very long silence, Lord Waterforde said:

"What I have to tell you two will come as a great surprise, but I hope you will understand."

Now Judy was trembling and Celita's fingers were even tighter than before.

"While you have both been away at School," Lord Waterforde was saying, "I found, Celita, that your Mother was very lonely and I did my best to keep her from brooding alone in the house."

"That was kind of you," Celita said. "I know how much Mama missed Papa. But she insisted on my going to Paris."

"And I insisted on Judy going, so I was very lonely too," Lord Waterforde said.

Again there was a strange silence before he went on with an obvious effort.

"We both hope that you will understand that as we are two people who are getting old, we need companionship. We therefore have decided that your Mother, Celita, will move into the Court so that I can look after her and see that she has everything she needs."

Celita looked at him in sheer astonishment.

"Move .. into .. Waterforde .. Court?" she murmured.

"Perhaps I should make it a little clearer," Lord Waterforde said. "Your Mother and I, Celita, were married last week very quietly in the Village Church, and now we are together and extremely happy."

For a moment both the girls were too astonished to move.

Then Judy jumped to her feet and ran to her father.

"If you have married the Countess, Papa, I am so very, very glad! I would have hated any Step-Mother to take Mama's place except her. She is so sweet and kind, and I know she will make you happy."

Lord Waterforde kissed his daughter and then found Celita beside him.

There were tears in her eyes as she said very quietly:

"Now I need not worry about Mama any more. It is also wonderful to think that we need not be afraid that you might turn us out."

"As if I would have ever done such a thing!" Lord Waterforde said indignantly.

Then he put his arm around Celita and hugged her.

"Your Mother was afraid you would be angry, and would think she had forgotten your Father. But I think your Father, who was my greatest friend, would have wanted me to look after someone he loved who was so very, very lonely."

"I am glad, so very, very glad, that you are now my Step-Father," Celita said. "I so often worried about Mama when I was in Paris. But now she will be safe and happy and, as you say, will have everything she needs."

"I will give her everything, including the moon and the stars thrown in," Lord Waterforde promised.

He gave a sigh as if a heavy weight had been lifted from his shoulders.

Then he added:

"Now, girls, you can tell me about yourselves and what has been happening here."

Celita looked at Judy.

Judy moved closer to her father.

"If you are happy, Papa," she said in a very small voice, "I am very happy too."

"You mean the *Duc* . . ." Lord Waterforde began.

". . . the *Duc* has fallen in love with Celita," Judy said, "and I am . . in love with . . Clive Cunningham."

Only Celita knew what a tremendous effort it had been for Judy to take the initiative.

She felt like applauding.

At the same time she waited anxiously to see Lord Waterforde's reaction.

For a moment he was astonished, as they had been astonished by his news.

Then he said:

"So the *Duc* is in love with Celita."

"It . . it . . was love . . at first sight," Celita said quickly.

It was wrong to lie, but she was determined not to upset him.

"And you, Judy?" Lord Waterforde enquired.

"I love Clive, Papa. And he is so clever with horses, just like you. I do not think I could be happy with any other man, and if I cannot marry Clive I shall just be an old maid until I die."

Lord Waterforde laughed.

'I am quite certain you will not be that! But I suppose if it is Clive you want, it is Clive you must have. Although I had hoped . . ."

He paused, and as if the thought had suddenly struck him, he said:

"If I cannot have the *Duc* de Sahran as my son-in-law, I can at least welcome him as my step-son-in-law!"

"Of course! That is what he will be!" Celita said. "And he is very thrilled and delighted at the thought of working with you on breeding and, of course, winning every Classic Race in Europe."

Lord Waterforde laughed.

"We must not set our sights too high to start with," he said, "but it is certainly something we will aim at for the future. Now let us go to tell the *Duc* and young Clive my good news, and I suppose I shall have to congratulate them on yours!"

Celita gave a deep sigh of relief.

Everything had turned out far better than she had dared to hope.

She knew it would be impossible now, if he was married to her Mother, for Lord Waterforde to make a scene about the *Duc* marrying her instead of Judy.

Judy had obviously got her own way in regard to Clive.

'This is wonderful! Wonderful!' she told herself, as they went to the Study to find the two men.

The *Duc's* eyes twinkled when he heard the news.

He insisted on opening a bottle of the best champagne for them to drink Lord Waterforde's health.

"You have beaten us to the post, My Lord!" he said. "Clive and I will expect you to drink our health when we are married."

"And please, Papa, can that be very soon?" Judy asked bravely. "We have been hearing about the beautiful house Clive is to have at Newmarket, and he and I will make your horses the most outstanding in the whole of England."

"I shall be very annoyed if you do not," Lord Waterforde said jokingly. "And of course you must have a very grand wedding. The whole County will want to come, and it will be a good opportunity for them to meet the *Duc* who is marrying my Step-Daughter."

Celita flashed a warning glance at the *Duc*.

This was something she had not expected.

She thought that if they had all that publicity about their engagement, it would make it more difficult to break it off later, and to say that they had changed their minds.

Lord Waterforde was obviously determined, if he could not

have the *Duc* exactly the way he wanted, to make the very best of the situation.

There were his horses, his marvellous Château which undoubtedly everyone would envy, and of course there were the ties with his family.

There was no possibility of their preventing Lord Waterforde from making plans.

He talked of their wedding and when it would take place until Lady Hilton arrived back.

"Oh here you are, Richard," she said. "I had no idea when I went out for the day that you were arriving. I am sorry that I was not here to greet you."

"I came to bring the girls news of what has been happening at home in their absence," Lord Waterforde said.

Then he told his sister that he was married to Celita's Mother.

She was astonished, and it was quite obvious that the idea that he might marry again had never entered her mind.

"I hope you will be very happy, Richard," she said at length.

There was unmistakably a slight reserve in her tone which said she suspected he had made a mistake.

However as the evening wore on, Celita realised that Lord Waterforde was very, very much in love with her mother.

He had obviously not been in love with his wife in the same way as the Countess had been with her husband.

But all that was best, kindest and most generous in his character was to be poured out at the feet of the Countess whom, Celita suspected, he had loved for a long time.

Perhaps even before her Father had died.

She was quite certain in her own mind that her Mother would never love any man in the same way as she had loved her Father.

Yet she was a very friendly and sociable person and liked having people around her.

Celita could understand that her mother found the long

months when she was at school, with no one to talk to in the house except the servants, extremely dismal.

Now she would be the Chatelaine of Waterforde Court and because Lord Waterforde liked entertaining, there would undoubtedly be luncheon and dinner parties every week.

When there was racing in the neighbourhood every bedroom would be filled.

"It is what Mama will enjoy," she told herself. "I am so very, very happy for her."

She could not help, however, feeling a little apprehensive about her own role in the future.

It was one thing to know that her Step-Father was delighted that the *Duc* wanted to marry her.

Quite another to fear that he would be annoyed, disappointed, and perhaps disagreeable when their engagement came to an end.

It was going to be very difficult, Celita thought in the darkness of her bedroom later that night.

The *Duc* would undoubtedly be continually coming to Waterforde Court, and Mama and Lord Waterforde would be travelling to France to stay at the Château.

She saw herself as a discarded fiancée being left behind.

She would be reproached for having lost the love and affection of such a great man.

It was too late now to think that they might have managed to make Lord Waterforde accept Clive without transferring the *Duc*, as it were, to her.

But for the moment it certainly made it easier if Lord Waterforde felt he was one of his family.

At the dinner-table he actually raised his glass and drank a toast to the *Duc* and Clive.

"We have been lucky! Very, very lucky," Celita told herself. "But we must not strain our luck too far. Unless the *Duc* is in a hurry to marry someone else, we must keep up our pretence until everything has settled down and Clive and Judy are happy in their Newmarket house."

She could not help hoping that she would be able to come

to the Château again before she and the *Duc* were supposed to change their minds and it was barred to her.

'It is so beautiful,' she thought, 'so lovely, and I have still not seen it all.'

She had been so thankful that everything had passed off so much better than she had feared that she had run to the Chapel before going upstairs to dress for dinner.

She felt she must say a prayer of gratitude.

The Chapel, built at the same time as the Château, was very beautiful.

The stained-glass windows and the carving were all of the same period.

Celita knelt down at the *prie-dieu* in front of the altar.

Raising her eyes up to the stained-glass window overhead, she thanked God fervently that Lord Waterforde was not angry.

In fact he had made her Mother very much happier than she had been since her Father died.

"Thank You .. Thank You, God," she said over and over again.

Then as she rose she realised she was not alone in the Chapel.

The *Duc* had come in through the Vestry door, and seeing her praying had stayed watching her.

Because she felt so happy, Celita held out her hand saying:

"I was thanking God, that everything went off so wonderfully. I am sure you were doing the same."

The *Duc* moved forward to take her hand in his.

Then he said:

"Actually I was asking Him, and I know you would approve, to find me the perfect wife which you tell me is essential."

"Then I know you will find her," Celita encouraged him. "One's prayers are always answered if one prays hard enough."

"I assure you I am praying very hard indeed," the *Duc* answered.

She realised that he was speaking seriously.

They moved together from the Chapel, along the corridor and into the Great Hall.

They came to the staircase and the *Duc* stopped.

"We have jumped the first fence," he said. "now it is just a question of passing the Winning Post in triumph."

"But of course you will do that," Celita smiled.

She ran up the stairs.

When she reached the top she looked back and saw the *Duc* was still watching her.

Chapter Six

The next morning the *Duc* took a great deal of trouble to arrange for Lord Waterforde to see first the stables, then the Race-course where his finest horses were to be on show.

"After luncheon," he said, "I will take you to see the mares."

This Celita knew was very important.

One of the reasons he needed Lord Waterforde as a partner was that he could not afford to extend his breeding-stables.

Clive and Judy were to accompany the *Duc* and Lord Waterforde.

As she thought it would be a mistake for her to be with them, Celita said:

"I want to write to Mama and tell her everything that has happened here and how pleased I am for her. So I shall not see you until luncheon time."

"Very well," the *Duc* agreed, "but I hope you will come with us in the afternoon."

She felt he was being polite.

Where the horses were concerned, she thought it best to leave everything to them and say as little as possible.

She appreciated that he was being very astute in including Clive in everything that concerned the horses.

It was obvious that Lord Waterforde had now accepted him as his future Son-in-Law.

At the same time it would be a mistake to push their luck too far, Celita thought.

She would not really feel happy about Judy until she and Clive were actually married.

Last night when she said "Good-night" to Lord Waterforde, he had said:

"I know your Mother is worrying about what I had to tell you. So let her know as soon as possible that, as far as you are concerned, everything is 'roses in the garden'."

Celita had smiled.

"I will tell her that, and I know it will make her happy."

"That is what I want her to be," Lord Waterforde said solemnly.

Then as if he somehow wanted to retrieve what he had lost he said:

"I have just been thinking. We will have a really grand wedding for you and Judy. Both of you married from the Court and of course fireworks in the garden for the tenants. We will ask the world to come to drink your health."

Celita had stood on tip-toe to kiss his cheek.

"It sounds marvellous," she said. "At the same time, while you are here you must concentrate on horses and nothing but horses, otherwise the *Duc* will be disappointed."

"I will not allow him to be that," Lord Waterforde promised, "and of course we will invite all his relations to stay for the wedding."

When she was alone in her bedroom, Celita thought over all that had been said.

Although Lord Waterforde would not have the *Duc* as a Son-in-Law, he was determined to make it obvious that they were very close.

She could almost hear him introducing with pride in his voice, "my Step-Daughter, The *Duchesse* de Sahran."

They might laugh and accept Lord Waterforde's obsession with titles.

But the moment must come first when she and the *Duc* parted.

What would Lord Waterforde say then?

However they had been so lucky that things had gone as well as they had.

At least she did not have Judy in tears.

She could only pray that nothing would happen until Judy was married to Clive and settled in their house at Newmarket.

The *Vicomte* also thought that he would be *de trop* while the *Duc* and Lord Waterforde discussed their future plans.

"I would like to go to Arles," he said, "If you will let me have a carriage to take me there. There is a very good saddler near the Cathedral. I want one or two things that I can buy better in Arles than I can buy anywhere else."

The *Duc* ordered a chaise for the *Vicomte* to drive himself, which he knew he would enjoy.

Then with a customary flurry, they set off.

The *Duc* lead the way to the stables where Lord Waterforde was to be very impressed by his horses.

Celita went to the Morning-Room which was especially at the disposal of visiting guests.

It is where they could snooze if they wanted to be quiet, or write their letters.

She sat down at an exquisite inlaid Writing-Desk which she guessed had been made in the reign of Louis XIV.

The *Duc* had heavily embossed writing-paper with his crest on it in red.

As she picked up her pen, Celita knew she must tell her Mother everything that had happened.

She started from the moment she left School.

She had written half-a-dozen sheets on both sides and still had a lot to say when a Maid came into the room.

She was a Maid who had occasionally waited on Celita since she had been at the Château.

She had noticed her particularly because, whenever she could, she spoke English.

"Have you been to England, Françoise?" she asked.

"No, M'Lady," the Maid had replied, "but I verry anxious do so."

Celita thought it was intelligent of her to try to learn English.

She had therefore spoken to her in that language whenever she appeared.

It was however, unusual for the Maids to come down to the ground floor.

When there was a message it was always brought by a Footman.

Françoise came to stand near the desk.

Celita finished the sentence she was writing and raised her head.

"What is it, Françoise?" she asked.

"There a Lady to see you, M'Lady," Françoise replied in French.

"A Lady!" Celita exclaimed. "Who can it be?"

"Someone very anxious meet you, M'Lady, and ask if you'll be very kind and speak with her. She has something very important to tell you."

Celita could not think what this could possibly be, or who could be calling to see her personally.

"Did the Lady give a name?" she enquired.

There was a moment's pause before Françoise shook her head.

Celita sighed.

"It is always the same. If one has something important to do, one is certain to be interrupted! Very well, Françoise, I will see this Lady, but I do hope she will not keep me long."

They left the Morning-Room and went into the Hall.

There was no one there except two Footmen.

Celita looked around.

"The Lady who called is in the garden," one of the Footmen volunteered.

Celita thought that was rather strange, but she walked out of the front door.

Then looking to the right she realised there was somebody on the lawn moving towards the French gardens.

"Is that the lady who wants to see me, Françoise?" she asked.

"Yes, yes, M'Lady," Françoise said in English.

Rather reluctantly, because she wanted to get on with her letter, she walked out into the sunshine.

She hurried towards the woman who had interrupted her.

To her surprise she still kept moving away.

By the time Celita actually caught up with her, she was half-way across the French garden.

Celita had somehow expected her to be a woman from Arles.

Perhaps this was a new way of selling some of the things which were made locally.

To her astonishment when she reached the woman in question she saw she was definitely a lady.

Very attractive, she was dressed in the latest fashion, and there were jewels glittering in her ears and round her neck.

Feeling breathless because she had hurried, Celita spoke first.

"I was told you wanted to see me," she said in French.

"That is correct," was the answer, "and I have indeed been very anxious to meet you, Lady – Celita – Dale."

She pronounced Celita's name slowly as if both words were difficult to say.

"May I know your name?" Celita enquired.

"I am Madame Yvonne Bédoin."

The name meant nothing to Celita, so she just smiled and waited for an explanation.

"You do not know me," Yvonne Bédoin said after a moment's pause, "but of course I have heard of you."

"I cannot think how you have done so," Celita said. "I hope you will not keep me long, as I have some very important letters to write."

"May I guess," Yvonne Bédoin said, "that you are writing home to your Mother to tell her of your engagement to the *Duc* de Sahran?"

Celita stared at her in astonishment.

"Why should you think that?" she asked after a moment.

"It is true, is it not?" Yvonne said. "Of course, Lady Celita, I must congratulate you on marrying such a charming and handsome man."

"Thank you," Celita said, "but for the moment our engagement is a secret because, as you are well aware, it will be for our families to be informed first."

It was the only thing she could think to say at the moment.

She was wondering how this strange woman who was so extremely smart, should be aware of her connection with the *Duc*.

They had managed to keep it a secret even from Lady Hilton who was staying in the house.

"Because I am an old friend of the *Duc's*," Yvonne Bédoin was saying, "I want to show you something very remarkable on his Estate which is, as it happens, known only to me."

Celita looked at her in surprise, and wondered what all this could be about.

"It is, in fact," Yvonne went on, "my Wedding present to you and to him, which I am sure you will find an interesting one."

"It is rather difficult to understand what you are saying," Celita said frankly.

Yvonne Bédoin gave a little tinkling laugh.

"That is true, but I am sure you will find what I have to show you thrilling, and so will the *Duc* when you share the secret with him."

"How can you know something here at the Château which he does not know?" Celita asked.

It was rather a blunt question, but she could not help thinking it was all quite bewildering.

How could this elegant woman be telling her something no one else knew?

"That is what I am going to explain," Yvonne Bédoin replied. 'You said you were busy, and so am I, as I am on my way back to Paris."

Celita thought she had been right in thinking this smartly dressed woman was not local.

Now she thought about it, she seemed to have Paris written all over her.

In her gown, and on her hat with its small feathers as a decoration.

She was wearing very exquisite long suede gloves, and very high-heeled shoes.

They made Celita wonder how she could walk swiftly over the grass lawn which was on the other side of the French garden.

In fact, Yvonne Bédoin walked so quickly that Celita found it difficult to continue their conversation.

They were going towards the cascade.

Now Celita could hear the roar of the water as it swept down from the small lake above into the basin surrounded by the Greek gods and goddesses.

"Are we going to the Cascade?" Celita managed to ask when it was still a little way ahead of them.

"That is right," Yvonne Bédoin replied, "and I will show you something the *Duc* does not know. When you show it to him, he will be delighted. Absolutely delighted!"

"It is a pity he is not here so you can show it to him at the same time," Celita said.

"Alas!" Yvonne Bédoin replied, "that is what I learnt when I arrived. But never mind! My Wedding present will be all the more acceptable because you give it into his hands either before or when you are his wife."

The way she spoke seemed rather odd.

Once again it struck Celita that it was extraordinary that someone from outside should know that she and the *Duc* were secretly engaged.

It was only yesterday that they had told Lord Waterforde and Lady Hilton about it.

She thought however it was no use asking questions.

It would only delay matters.

As soon as she saw what this strange woman wanted her to

see, the quicker she would be able to go back to the Château and finish her letter.

They reached the Cascade.

As it roared down into the basin, it stirred the water as it fell.

Shimmering in the sunshine, it swept slowly towards the far end from which it fell down into the gorge.

To Celita's surprise Yvonne Bédoin went to the side of the Cascade.

Reaching up she turned what looked like a key.

It was obscured by the thick creeper that covered the rock-wall beside it.

It took Yvonne Bédoin a moment or two to manipulate the key.

By the side of the Cascade, a very narrow door opened.

It was then that Celita realised for the first time that it was possible to go behind the Cascade itself.

She had heard of it happening in other places.

It had never struck her when the *Duc* had shown her the Cascade that it might be possible to go behind it.

She wanted to ask many questions.

However, having opened the door, Yvonne Bédoin stepped through the narrow entrance.

Then she turned round, beckoning to Celita to follow her.

She managed to do so without getting wet.

She found herself in what appeared to be a huge cavern behind the Cascade.

The light was coming in iridescent through the water and the roar of it seemed to be quite deafening.

Very wisely Yvonne Bédoin had stepped back from the Cascade itself.

There was no fear of being splashed and she was standing some way in on a dry floor.

Piled together on one side of the cavern, were the broken bodies of the statues which had been replaced.

Celita looked round.

There did not seem to be much else except that the Cavern went back a long way.

She wondered what was the Wedding present she was to give the *Duc*.

He would obviously know of the entrance behind the Cascade.

There did not seem to be anything else unusual about where they were.

Yvonne Bédoin came towards her and said:

"Look at the water and tell me what you see."

Wonderingly, Celita did as she was told.

Although the water poured and went on pouring, there did not seem anything particular to notice.

Suddenly Yvonne Bédoin said:

"Put your hands out behind you, quickly!"

Because she spoke sharply, Celita did as she was told.

She wondered why she should do so, and if she was to receive something to hold in a somewhat strange way.

Then she felt Yvonne Bédoin's hands touch first one wrist and then the other.

She was suddenly aware, although it seemed incredible, that the French woman had roped her wrists together.

"What are you doing?" Celita asked. "Whatever is happening?"

Celita tried to turn round, but before she could do so, she was aware a rope was being put round her ankles and that too was tied tightly.

"What are . . you doing?" Celita demanded again.

Now that her ankles were tied Yvonne Bédoin rose to her feet.

"You," she said, "are my Wedding present to the *Duc*! I doubt if they will find you here before you are dead. Remember, as you die, that he made me unhappy. This is the way I repay him for the manner in which he has treated me."

She had to speak the words loudly above the roar of the Cascade.

As she finished speaking she turned.

Swirling her skirts, she walked to the entrance and slipped through it.

"Wait! Wait! What .. are you .. saying?" Celita cried out.

She was too late!

She had been so astonished by what the French Woman had said that she realised she had let her go without protesting.

She heard the door close and the key turn in the lock.

Then there was only the roar of the Cascade.

It took Celita some minutes to realise she was imprisoned.

Tied hand and foot, she was in a place where the *Duc* would never find her.

He had never said a word, when they had looked at the Cascade together, about being able to go behind it.

He would certainly not suspect a stranger like herself to find her way there.

Celita strained at the rope which held her hands.

It was a thin cord, tied very skilfully, which it was impossible for her to stretch or break it.

"What can I do?" she asked desperately. "What can I do?"

There was nothing to sit on except the broken bodies of the Greek gods.

She could not walk towards them.

She managed however to get there by jumping.

She had to be careful not to fall over.

If she did she would doubtless hurt herself on the hard ground.

By making a series of little jumps, and waiting to get her breath before she took another, she gradually reached the statues.

She sat down, aware that her arms were getting stiff.

She looked down at what she was sitting on.

She realised that the head of one of the statues had been broken off sharply.

It had left a sharp jagged edge on the stone from which it had been carved.

It took Celita some time to manage to sit with her back to

it, and to get the raw edge of the stone against the rope tying her wrists.

She rubbed it up and down, up and down, up and down.

It took so long to break she had begun to think it was impossible, when suddenly it gave.

She was so relieved she almost cried.

At the same time her arms were exhausted.

For a few minutes she could only sit limply, getting her breath.

Gradually the blood circulated back into her wrists where the rope had been tied so tightly.

But her hands were free and now she was able to release her legs.

As she started to do so, she realised she was hungry.

By now it must be long after luncheon-time.

They would have come back from the Race-Course and would wonder where she was.

Françoise had said she did not know the name of the lady who had called.

The *Duc* would probably think it might be someone who had come to dance the previous evening.

Or perhaps an unknown friend from England who had turned up unexpectedly.

"How can I get out of this horrible place, and tell them what has happened?" Celita wondered.

She rubbed her ankles because they too had suffered from the tightness of the rope Yvonne Bédoin had used.

She rubbed them until the circulation was restored and then got to her feet.

She managed to get to the door through which they had entered the cavern.

One look at it and Celita's heart sank.

It was strongly made.

In fact exceptionally strongly, in case it should rot from the water pouring down beside it.

The lock, which was right above her head, was, she could see, a very strong one.

It was quite impossible for her to operate it from the inside.

If she could not leave the Cavern that way, there was only one other.

That was through the Cascade itself.

She looked at it pouring down and shuddered.

If she tried to throw herself through it, she had the feeling she would be held down in the water.

She could not swim.

By the time she came to the surface she would doubtless be unconscious, if not already drowned.

It was something she dared not risk.

She now wondered despairingly what else she could do.

There was just the Cascade, and the long Cavern seemed to be blocked at the far end.

It was light enough for her to see that there were a few pieces of wood.

They might have been used when the men were changing over the statues.

There was nothing else except what appeared to be a wall of large white bricks.

It covered the end of the Cavern.

Although it did not reach the roof it had obviously been built for some reason.

Perhaps to strengthen the Cavern against the water overhead.

That meant, of course, there was no way for her to escape through the roof of the Cavern.

It would only bring her into the small lake into which the water fed as it poured down from the mountains.

"What can I do? What can I do?" Celita asked. "Please God . . help me!"

She leant against the wall as she spoke.

Then she realised that the bricks had become loose with age, and as she pushed one it tumbled onto the floor.

It struck her that perhaps if she threw bricks through the Cascade it might attract someone's attention.

But who was likely to be staring at the Cascade in the middle of the afternoon?

In any case a brick coming through the water would be gone almost instantly to the bottom of the basin.

She pulled another brick which was loose and wondered vaguely if there was anything behind it.

Then to her surprise she felt wood.

Because by now she was getting desperate and was very frightened, she pulled away several more bricks.

The mortar with which they had been joined together had rotted, so that they were quite loose.

Then as she cleared away some of the rubble, she found she was right in thinking it was wood.

Because she felt in some way this might help her, although she had no idea how, she removed some more bricks.

Then she found she was looking at the top of a wooden packing-case.

She thought it must be locked.

But she found the lid was only joined to the side by a hinge.

She opened it.

To her astonishment she saw the packing-case was filled to the top with articles that were wrapped up.

This was what she had hoped.

Picking up the first thing that came to hand, which was rolled up in a linen napkin, she unwrapped it.

She found herself looking at a gold drinking-vase.

It glinted in the light.

When she looked at the napkin a little closer, she saw that it had embroidered on it the *Duc's* coat-of-arms.

For a moment she could only gasp.

What she guessed she had found was so tremendous she could hardly believe it was true.

Then she was feeling into the packing-case, pulling out one thing after another.

First a gold plate, then another gold cup, gold spoons and more plates of every size.

Each one was wrapped in a napkin and she knew this gave her a chance of survival.

She put the gold cups and plates back into the case.

Picking up an armful of the napkins, she walked towards the cascade.

She tried to throw the first one but the water swept it back on to the floor beside her.

She then realised that she had to have a better plan.

Going back to the wall, she collected some bricks.

She wrapped a brick in a napkin and threw it with all her strength through the Cascade.

She knew it would reach the other side and hoped that, while the brick would sink to the bottom, the napkin would float.

Someone, surely someone would see the napkins floating on the surface of the basin and think it strange?

It was quite hard work, throwing the bricks one after another through the heavy fall of water.

Finally she had thrown the very last of the napkins.

Then she went back to the bricked-up wall and pulled away more loose bricks.

Finally she found another large case very like the one she had discovered first.

In this case there were the gold candelabra that must have been on the Dining-Room table.

There was also exquisitely made gold goblets, set with huge precious stones.

At any other time Celita would have been thrilled to examine each one.

But all she wanted at the moment was what they were wrapped in.

To her delight they were too large for the napkins.

Instead the candelabra were wrapped in table-cloths.

Some of the gold goblets were in red velvet covers from which the cushions had been removed.

Someone must see this, Celita thought desperately.

Carefully she threw them one by one through the Cascade.

As she did so she was aware the sun was sinking and soon it would be dark.

She must have failed in her effort to attract attention she told herself miserably.

What she had thrown through the Cascade and into the basin must have sunk to the bottom or had been carried so quickly into the gorge beyond that no one had noticed them.

She sat down again on the body of the god who had helped her to get her hands free.

She thought that she could do no more.

"Save me! Save me!" she had cried in her heart as she had thrown first the napkins then the other cloths through the Cascade.

"Surely," she thought, "the *Duc* must hear me calling him."

She remembered that sometimes they could read each others thoughts.

She had known what he was feeling without his having to say anything.

Just as he had looked into her eyes and known what she was thinking.

"Come and . . save me! Oh . . come . . and save . . me!" she called out to him with her whole heart.

She hoped that wherever he was, however much he was absorbed in his horses, he would realise she wanted him.

She almost felt she could see him.

He was looking so handsome, laughing at something that had been said, or planning the future.

He had a look which told her all too clearly he intended to get his own way.

He would not only be saving her.

If he knew what she had found, he would realise he would be saving himself.

He would not have to dependent on Lord Waterforde or anyone else.

She had been put here to die.

But she had found the gold dinner-service which he had told her was the finest in France.

She was quite certain that the other cases, and there were many of them, would contain the Sahran jewels, and other treasures that had been saved in this clever way from being looted in the Revolution.

It must, she thought, have been done by the faithful servants they had left behind.

The family themselves had fled to escape the guillotine.

The reason they had never known what had happened would be that the servants themselves had lost their lives in trying to save the Château from the Revolutionaries.

It was all a wonderful, wonderful story.

Yet if the *Duc* did not find her before she was dead, he would never know what she had discovered for him, and him alone.

"Oh . . René! René!" She called in her heart.

"Come . . and . . save me . . I . . want . . you!"

. . . .

The *Duc* came back with his guests for luncheon in a very good mood.

Lord Waterforde had been delighted with the horses and even more with the Race-Course.

The *Duc* had had his finest Race-Horse parading.

He and Clive had taken the others over the jumps.

Lord Waterforde had certainly been impressed, and when they got back to the Château, was full of congratulations to the *Duc*, and incidentally to himself.

Judy ran upstairs to tidy herself before luncheon.

When she came down to find her Father and the *Duc* having a glass of champagne, she said:

"I wonder where Celita is. She must know we are back by now."

The *Duc* looked at his watch.

"It is after half past one," he said. "I was rather afraid she would be getting hungry."

"I am certainly hungry!" Clive said as he came into the room. "I have never jumped so high in my whole life."

"You were magnificent, my boy," Lord Waterforde said.

The way he spoke told Clive that because of his horsemanship, he had definitely been accepted into the Waterforde family.

The *Duc* made enquiries, but no one could find Celita and they went into luncheon.

He did not worry about her as he thought she must have gone out for a walk.

Then after luncheon he went into the Morning-Room and saw her unfinished letter to her mother.

That seemed to him rather strange.

Although he knew her so little, he was quite certain she was a very tidy person.

If she set herself a task, he knew she would finish it.

On an impulse he went upstairs into her Bedroom.

It was obvious she was not there.

Nor, he thought, had she been there since the bed had been made and the room tidied.

"Where can she be?" he asked.

At three o'clock there was still no sign of Celita.

Lord Waterforde was anxious to go to see the Mares.

The *Duc* had to force himself to do what was wanted, even though he was worried.

In fact he hurried Lord Waterforde through his inspection of the mares and brought him back to the Château much more quickly than he had intended.

There was English Tea prepared for the English guests in the Drawing-Room.

By this time the *Duc* was really worried.

He also had the strange feeling that Celita wanted him.

He could not explain it to himself, but he knew he could hear her calling him.

There was a little catch in her breath as she did so, as if she was frightened.

"What can have happened? What the devil can have happened?" he asked.

He went into the Hall and spoke to the Major Domo.

"I cannot imagine," he said, "what has happened to Lady Celita. When did anyone here see her last?"

"I was told," the Major Domo replied, "only a short while ago, *Monsieur*, that a Lady called to see Lady Celita this morning."

"A Lady?" the *Duc* asked.

"Yes, *Monsieur*. But she asked for one of the Maids, and it as she who took Her Ladyship to the caller who was in the garden."

"I do not understand what is happening," the *Duc* said. "Fetch me the maid!"

He went into his Study.

He was annoyed that it took nearly four minutes before Françoise appeared.

"What is your name?" he enquired.

"Françoise, *Monsieur le Duc*," Françoise said, making a curtsy.

"How long have you been here in the Château?"

"A month, *Monsieur*."

"Only a month?" the *Duc* asked. "Why?"

"I was very anxious to come here, *Monsieur*."

"And where have you come from?"

"Paris, *Monsieur*."

"I understand that today a Lady called who wished to see one of my guests, and the Lady, whoever she was asked for you!"

"*Oui, Monsieur*."

"Did you know this Lady before you came here?"

There was a long pause and when Françoise said "No!" the *Duc* knew she was lying.

"I want you to tell me the truth," he said sharply. "So I will repeat that question. Did you know the Lady who called today, and what was her name?"

"I . . it . . was *Madame* Yvonne Bédoin, *Monsieur le Duc*."

The *Duc* drew in his breath.

"Am I right in thinking it was *Madame* Bédoin who got you the position here in the Château?"

"*Oui, Monsieur.*"

"I presume she wrote to the House-Keeper?"

"*Oui, Monsieur.*"

"So when *Madame* Bédoin came here this morning, she sent for you?"

"*Oui, Monsieur.*"

"Now, Françoise," the *Duc* said, "I want you to tell me the truth. If you do not tell me the truth, I shall know it and I shall take steps to make it very unpleasant and very uncomfortable for you. Do you understand?"

"*Oui, Monsieur.*"

Françoise was now trembling.

The *Duc* said:

"Tell me what *Madame* Bédoin said when she arrived."

"She sent for me, *Monsieur*, and told me I was to ask Lady Celita to meet her in the garden."

"In the garden!" the *Duc* exclaimed.

"*Oui, Monsieur.*"

"And Lady Celita did so?"

"*Oui, Monsieur.*"

"And what happened?"

"I do not know, *Monsieur*. I promise you I do not know. Lady Celita ran down to where *Madame* Bédoin was waiting for her.'

"And where was that?"

"Just before where the lawn goes to the Cascade."

"And did you see *Madame* Bédoin after that?"

"*Oui, Monsieur le Duc*. She came back to the Château . . .'

"Alone?" the *Duc* interrupted.

"Alone, *Monsieur*."

"And what happened?"

"She sent for her carriage and left."

"And what time was that?"

"I think about 11.30., *Monsieur*."

"And you did not see Lady Celita come back?"

"*Non, Monsieur*, and that is the truth. I did not see her again."

The *Duc* got up from the desk at which he had been sitting and walked out of the room.

He went quickly through the Hall into the garden.

He could not believe that Yvonne had physically attacked Celita.

But anything was possible with a woman who was jealous, as she was jealous of him.

As he moved through the French Garden, he could feel Celita calling him again.

Now he was sure she had called him during the afternoon.

If she was calling him, then she must be alive.

Where could she possibly be?

The French Garden came to an end and he stepped on to the well-kept ground which led down to the Cascade.

He had almost reached it when he saw one of his Gardeners, an old man who had been with him for some years.

He was coming from the end of the basin where the statues were.

He saw the *Duc* and hurried towards him.

"I was coming to see you, *Monsieur, le Duc*," he said.

He was holding something in his hand and he held it out to the *Duc*.

"This was floating in the basin," he said, "and there're many more of them. I can't think where they've come from."

The *Duc* put out his hand.

For one horrifying moment he thought what he was touching was a part of Celita's clothes.

If it was from the basin, she was dead.

Then he was aware that it was a napkin and he saw his own Coat-of-Arms.

"You found this floating in the basin?" he asked.

The Gardener turned round to point.

"Look! *Monsieur*. Look! There are many of them."

The *Duc* saw he was right.

There were napkins forced by the water to the far end of the basin where it fell down into the gorge.

He looked at them and then at the Cascade.

Even as he looked at the falling water he saw something red come through the centre of it and fall into the water.

It was churned down and then up again, until it was floating on the water.

It was then the *Duc* began to run towards the Cascade and the Gardener followed him.

He reached the door.

He put up his hand to find the key which was always left in the lock.

He had given orders because he thought it was a mistake for people to keep going behind the Cascade, than no one was to go in there.

The key, however was ready for the gardeners if they had to clean out the basin.

As he well knew, the door could not be opened without it.

It was then he knew where Celita was and who had put her there.

Turning to the gardener he said:

"Go at once, and find the Estate Carpenter. Tell him to come here at once with his tools. We cannot open the door as the key is missing."

There was no doubt from the way the *Duc* spoke that he was in a hurry.

The man turned and old though he was, started to run back towards the Château.

The *Duc* stood looking at the lock.

He was sure that Celita was inside and praying that he would come to her.

Now he was nearer he could almost feel her vibrations moving out towards his.

Then he turned to look at the flower-bed at the side of the Cascade.

It was almost as if he was being guided.

He saw the key flash in the last light of the sun before it sank behind the distant mountains.

He picked it up and opened the door.

As it swung open he was almost afraid to go in, afraid of what he might find.

Then as he stepped forward Celita came from the shadows.

"You .. have .. come! You .. have .. come! I prayed .. you would .. understand. Oh .. you have .. come to .. save me!"

She flung herself against him and the *Duc's* arms went round her.

Then his lips were on hers.

He was kissing her wildly, possessively, passionately because he thought he might have lost her.

Chapter Seven

The *Duc* raised his head and looked down at Celita.

She was staring up at him, her eyes radiant with an expression in them he had never seen before.

Then as if he could not help himself, he asked in a strangely deep voice:

"How can you do this to me?"

Then he was kissing her again.

Kissing her until Celita felt they were flying in the sky and her feet were no longer on earth.

She could not believe it was true that the *Duc* was kissing her!

He evoked in her feelings she had never known before, but which she knew were love.

Only when once again his lips left hers did she say as if she could not help herself.

"I . . love . . you!"

"And I love you," the *Duc* said. "I have loved you since the first moment I saw you, but I knew you did not love me."

He pulled her almost roughly closer to him as he said:

"I prayed in the way that you pray that you would love me. And when I saw you holding that baby in your arms yesterday, I knew you were the perfect woman you told me to find."

"Is that . . true? Is that . . really . . true?" Celita asked.

Her voice seemed to come from a long distance.

It did not sound very coherent, but the *Duc* understood.

"You know it is true," he said. "You have told me to seek

perfection and I found it with you. I love you, and no one shall take you from me."

The agony he had felt when he thought she was dead swept through him again, and he said:

"How could you have been so clever in telling me where you were hidden? But when I saw what the gardener had fished out of the water, I thought you were dead."

She knew by the pain in his voice how terrified he had been for her.

She moved to lay her face against his shoulder.

"I am .. not .. dead, I am .. alive!" she said. "And .. now that you have .. kissed me I want to .. live because love is so .. wonderful."

"Very, very wonderful," the *Duc* agreed.

Once again his lips were seeking hers.

Before he could kiss her Celita put up her fingers to prevent him.

"I have something to tell you. Something marvellous which will make you very happy."

"You have already made me happy," he said. "You are everything I have wanted but, as you know, I have been disappointed. But now I have found you, I will never, never let you go."

He spoke defiantly, as if he was challenging the world to take her from him.

Celita moved in his arms.

"Come and see what I have to show you," she begged.

It was growing dark but it was still light enough for them to see their way to the back of the cave.

The *Duc* was thinking how he had barred everyone from going behind the Cascade.

Only Celita would have been intelligent enough to attract attention by throwing material into the basin.

It surprised him that there had been anything she could throw.

He wondered how the table-napkins had got there.

They reached the brick wall and Celita moved ahead of him.

She put her hand down into the second packing-case she had opened.

She pulled out one of the golden goblets that was set with precious stones.

She held it up towards the light and said:

"I think this is what you have been looking for."

The *Duc* stared at it in astonishment.

Then, as if he could not believe it was real, he put out his hand to touch it.

"Where has this come from?" he asked. "It must be part of the treasures that were stolen during the Revolution."

"Not stolen," Celita said. "They were hidden here so that eventually you would find them."

The *Duc* bent over the packing-case and pulled out more goblets.

Then he moved to the first one from which Celita had taken the napkins and found the gold plates.

"I do not believe it!" he exclaimed. "These have been here the whole time I have been bemoaning their loss."

"There are other cases I have not opened," Celita said. "I was just trying to find material which would tell you where I was."

"It was a long time before you thought of that?" the *Duc* asked.

He remembered that he had not really been worried until late in the afternoon.

There was a moment's pause then Celita said:

"*Madame* Bédoin .. tied me up .. and it was .. very difficult for .. me to .. get lose."

"Tied you up?" the *Duc* asked incredulously.

Celita pointed to where the ropes with which she had been tied lay on the floor.

"It was one of your .. gods or .. goddesses who .. saved me," she said. "I managed to .. rub the rope .. against the broken neck .. until it snapped."

The *Duc's* lips tightened.

He thought only a woman like Yvonne Bédoin would have thought of anything so cruel.

Only jealousy would make any woman rope a young girl to make her immobile and leave her to die in a place where she would never be found.

He remembered all too vividly bringing Yvonne as a visitor to the Château.

She had insisted that she must see it.

When she arrived, he had taken her over to the Cascade.

She had been very intrigued with it.

She insisted on going behind it because it was something she had done in Germany.

"When the wind blows," the *Duc* had explained to her, "it becomes very wet and slippery inside the cave, I have therefore forbidden anyone on the Estate to use the door without my permission."

"That is very sensible of you," Yvonne had remarked. "But I want to see that water from behind, and I think, René dear, that you will agree that it makes a very appropriate background for me."

She stood posed with the waterfall running behind her.

She was well aware that it accentuated the white of her skin, her dark hair and her flashing eyes.

The *Duc* also knew without her saying so, that she was imagining how she would look naked in front of the water.

Because he had no wish to take part in such a charade in the privacy of his own home, he hurried her away.

He could understand that because he had left her she wanted to hurt Celita.

In fact to annihilate her so that she could not marry him.

It was then she must have remembered the Cascade.

She had known that if Celita was imprisoned there she would die of starvation and cold.

No one would imagine that she would find herself behind the Cascade.

The *Duc* could only thank God that Celita had had the

intelligence to free herself and to think of a way of attracting attention.

He put his arms around her and held her close.

"You have not only saved yourself," he said, "but given me back my fortune. How can it be possible for me to live without you?"

"You are quite .. sure you .. want .. me?" Celita asked.

"It will take me at least eight hundred years to tell you how much," he said. "And on the eight hundredth anniversary of our wedding you shall tell me that I was right."

Celita laughed.

"I shall be wondering all that time," she said, "whether .. you are .. happy with me or .. missing the *amusements* of Paris."

"That is something again we will discuss on our anniversary," he said.

They were laughing as the door by the Cascade was pushed further open.

The Estate Carpenter and two of the gardeners came hurrying in.

"You are just the men I want to see," the *Duc* said. "Fortunately I found the key, but I have also discovered, or rather Lady Celita discovered for me, that some of the most valuable treasures from the Château were hidden here during the Revolution. No one had the slightest idea where they were."

The Estate Carpenter looked behind him and gave an exclamation.

"I thought that brick wall, *Monsieur le Duc*," he said, "was part of the cave."

"That is what we all thought," the *Duc* answered. "Instead as you can see, it concealed a number of packing-cases. First thing tomorrow morning I want them brought up to the Château.

He shut the top of the packing-case nearest to him and said:

"Close them and hammer them down before you bring

them from here. I trust you not to talk to anyone else on the Estate until they are safely inside the Château itself."

The men understood that he was afraid of thieves and nodded their heads.

"Lady Celita and I are now going back," the *Duc* said. "Lock the door and keep the key with you for the night.

He was talking to the Chief Carpenter who assured the *Duc* he would do that.

Then the *Duc* and Celita started to walk back towards the Château.

By now the first evening stars were out in the sky.

The last glow of crimson was sinking down behind the great trees.

Yet the fountains still caught a glimmer of it.

They seemed to Celita to give her a special welcome as she walked towards the Château.

She now held a very different place in the *Duc's* life than when she had left it.

She could hardly believe it was true that he loved her.

She knew she loved him.

But she had not realised before that what she felt was love.

Never having been in love, she was very innocent.

The feelings she had had when with him had not been recognisable.

Yet she knew now that, when she wanted to talk to him, when she loved arguing with him or, as he said, 'duelling in words', and when he smiled at her, she had really felt her heart leap.

It had been because they were getting closer and closer to each other.

"Now I am part of him," she told herself, "and when we are married I shall know what love means."

She looked up at him and she knew once again that he was reading her thoughts.

"You told me I should find what I was seeking," he said, "and I have lain awake at night wondering how I could ever make you understand it was you."

"It was stupid of me not to realise I would fall in love with you," Celita said, "and very stupid of you not to realise it was inevitable."

The *Duc's* eyes were twinkling.

"Now you are making me feel conceited," he said. "I do not expect every woman I meet to fall in love with me."

"I am determined to make certain you do not escape, and now I am yours – hook, line and sinker," Celita teased. "So I hope you will be very careful of me."

"You can be quite sure of that," the *Duc* said.

.   .   .   .

When she appeared in the Drawing-Room the others gave a cry of relief.

"Where have you been? What has happened?" Judy asked.

Celita had already thought it would be a mistake to mention Yvonne Bédoin, but before she could speak the *Duc* replied.

"Celita was being too adventurous. She found her way behind the Cascade, but the door shut and she could not find a way out."

"Oh, poor Celita! how terrible for you!" Judy cried. "But now you are safe and I am sure you are hungry."

"I am, as it happens," Celita said. "I am sure you all ate a delicious dinner without worrying about me."

"As a matter of fact," the *Vicomte* said, "we have only just finished, and as René has had nothing to eat I expect that the Chef is waiting for you to go into the Dining-Room."

"That is exactly where we will go," the *Duc* said. "We will come back later and tell you more of Celita's adventures, but, thank God, for the moment they are over."

"I remember," Lord Waterforde said, as if he wanted to say something of importance, "Celita, as a child, was always exploring places that were otherwise private. And there were innumerable occasions when her Nurse, or later a Governess, could not find her."

"I think on those occasions," Celita laughed, "I was always in the stables. I used to crouch down and hide in the stalls when they came looking for me."

"Well, in future keep to the stables," Lord Waterforde advised, "and then we shall know where you are."

The *Duc* drew Celita towards the Dining-Room.

When they were out of earshot of the others, he said:

"That was much more sensible than letting them know too much."

"I am only hoping," Celita said, "that all the other ladies who have loved you and whom you have abandoned, do not wish to kill me! Otherwise I shall have to employ a bodyguard."

"That will be me!" the *Duc* declared. "I have no intention of ever letting you out of my sight for a moment. So how soon will you marry me?"

He sat down at the table as he made the last remark.

Celita thought that it was not the usual place at which one heard a proposal of marriage.

But then everything about the *Duc* was different from the ordinary.

"I am not being romantic," he went on, "I am being practical. I am certainly not going to wait while His Lordship arranges this pageant on which he has set his heart, with people throwing rose petals all the way from the Church, and thousands of hands to shake, before we can be alone!"

Celita laughed and made a rather hopeless gesture with her hands.

"You know he will want to show you off!" she said.

"If he does, it will rather take the limelight off Judy," the *Duc* said.

"I had thought of that," Celita said. "But of course what I was really wondering was how we could manage to quarrel and part so that you could gain your freedom and start looking for your Heiress."

"I have found my Heiress!" the *Duc* said. "And with her

dowry that no other woman in the world could bring to her marriage."

Celita knew he was referring to the treasure she had found in the cave.

The *Duc* said after a moment:

"Unless I am very much mistaken, at least one of the packing-cases will be filled with nothing but gold Louis."

Celita stared at him.

"How do you know that?"

"I have a list of what was in the safes at the Château when my family had to leave at a moment's notice. They had heard officials of the Revolution were on their way from Paris to bring them to the Seat of Justice, which of course meant that they would be guillotined."

"So they ran away?" Celita said.

"Very wisely," the *Duc* replied. "They reached Marseilles and went to live in Africa. That is why, I think, my Grandfather was never told what had happened to the treasures that were left behind."

He paused for a moment before he went on:

"I have been thinking that it must have been the old and most trusted servants who hid them where you found them. Then of course they left the Château themselves and, I suspect, died before imparting their secret to anyone."

"And you think there was a lot of money as well as the ornaments which we have seen?" Celita asked.

"Money," the *Duc* said, "and the jewellery that had accumulated down the centuries. It was always said to be better than anything owned by the Kings of France."

He smiled before he said:

"You will look very lovely in it, my Darling."

Another course was handed to them and finally the servants withdrew leaving the *Duc* with a small glass of brandy.

As the door into the Pantry shut, the *Duc* said;

"Now, my Precious, tell me how I can marry you without there being a row about it, and without my having to wait and become the performing clown to please your Step-Father."

There was silence for a moment and then Celita said:

"There is one thing he has not taken into account, and that is that you are a catholic."

"Of course," the *Doc* said. "Perhaps that will let me escape the actual Marriage Service, if nothing else."

Celita did not speak and after a moment he said:

"What I would like more than anything else, is that we should marry here in my Chapel and spend a little of our honeymoon alone before we go to England for Judy's Wedding."

He saw just a touch of surprise in Celita's eyes at his last words, and he said:

"I think we should support them. And if your Step-Father wishes to produce the *Duc* and *Duchesse* de Sahran like a pair of rabbits out of a hat, let him!"

Celita laughed.

"You are wonderful!" she said. "Only you could understand how much he wants to do that and how happy it will make him."

"Very well," the *Duc* said. "I will play my part with a false smile. But I want my own way first."

"I will tell you something which I think will please you," Celita asked.

"What is it?" the *Duc* said.

"I was Baptised a Catholic."

The *Duc* stared at her.

"How is that possible, when I know your Father and mother are Protestants?"

"When Papa and Mama were married they went on a long honeymoon," Celita began. "Papa wanted to show my Mother the parts of the world that he particularly loved. This included Greece, Constantinople, and Greece."

"That is where I will take you," the *Duc* said.

Celita smiled at him and then went on:

"They had, Mama said, a glorious time, but there was some muddle over their return journey from Alexandria, and they were therefore delayed in Egypt longer than they intended. I was on the way and when the ship reached Malta I was born prematurely."

The *Duc* was listening attentively.

"That would not have happened," Celita explained, "if in climbing up and down in the various Churches Mama had not slipped, and after Papa had picked her up, he hurriedly took her to the nearest Convent."

"That was sensible!" the *Duc* murmured.

"The Nuns brought me into the world," Celita went on, "and because I was only a seven-month baby and very small, they thought I must die. So a Priest was hastily brought to the Convent and Baptised me. I was given the name of Mary – the Mother of God."

"And that is exactly how you looked," the *Duc* explained, "when you were holding the Farmer's little boy in your arms, and how you will look, my Darling, when you hold my son."

Celita put out her hand to touch his before she went on:

"Of course, when we got back to England I was Baptised in the Family Church and given the name of Celita. My Father never referred to my first Baptism, but Mama told me about it when I was older and she actually showed me the Certificate signed by the Priest who Baptised me."

The *Duc* drew in a deep breath.

"That solves everything! As Judy said so truly, you, my precious one, always have an answer to everything."

"What do you mean?" Celita enquired.

"Lord Waterforde was saying today when you were missing," the *Duc* explained, "that he intended to take you and Judy home the day after tomorrow. He shall certainly take Judy with him. You, as my wife, will stay behind with me."

"You are going to tell him that we are to be married?" Celita asked.

The *Duc* shook his head.

"No, he will talk about it, argue about it, and that, my precious, will spoil the wonder and glory of it for you and me."

He put his finger up to his forehead saying:

130

"Now let me think. Tomorrow he will want to ride and talk even more about the horses than he has already. But I will arrange that as they will be leaving at ten o'clock the next morning, we will dine early."

He was obviously working it out in a rather complicated way so Celita did not interrupt.

She was thinking she would always be able to rely on him to arrange things in the future.

Whatever he wanted she wanted, and that she told herself was the foundation of a happy marriage.

"What we will do," the *Duc* went on, "is we will be married in the Chapel at nine o'clock tomorrow evening. My private Chaplain will perform the Service, and there will be nobody there except Gustav who will give you away, and also be my Best man."

Celita made a little sound but did not interrupt.

"We will make some excuse to leave the rest after Dinner and later Gustav will go back and say that we were very tired and have therefore retired early."

The *Duc* drew in a deep breath.

"Then we shall be alone," he finished very quietly. "Lord Waterforde, Judy and Cunningham will leave at ten o'clock. You will stay with me as my wife."

"You are quite .. certain we .. can do .. that?" Celita asked.

"Quite, quite certain," the *Duc* answered. "It just needs organisation. There will be no time for anyone to be disagreeable or to find fault. We will have given orders not to be disturbed and Gustav will give Lord Waterforde a letter from me explaining everything. You will finish your letter to your Mother. I think she will understand."

"I do hope so," Celita murmured.

"She will!" the *Duc* said firmly. "They will still be gasping as they drive away, so as not to miss the train from Arles. You and I my lovely one will be here alone before I take you to a very special place high up in the hills where I have a Château, small compared with this one, but just made for lovers."

Celita's eyes were shining.

"You are .. wonderful," she said. "You think of .. everything."

Then as the *Duc* bent across to kiss her she told herself that only a magician could be so clever.

. . . .

They had laughed a great deal at dinner at the jokes the *Duc* and Gustav exchanged with each other.

Then as the Ladies rose to lead the way to the Drawing-Room, the *Duc* said:

"I have some papers that have to be signed and I would be grateful if you, Celita, and you, Gustav, could witness them for me."

"Yes, of course," they both said.

"We will not be very long," the *Duc* said to Lord Waterforde, "but I have put some presents for you in in the Drawing-Room as momentoes of your visit here. One very special one is also a Wedding Present for your wife."

"You are very kind," Lord Waterforde said. "I know she will appreciate it."

"There is also a present for Clive," the *Duc* added, "which will keep you amused for several hours."

"Now you are making me curious," Lord Waterforde smiled.

He seemed to hurry towards the Drawing-Room.

Celita had already been let into the secret that this was a board-game.

Those taking part each had a horse that had to complete a Race-Course, taking jump after jump.

Only, of course, if they could throw the right number on the dice.

When the *Duc* had shown it to her she thought that it was very intriguing.

She was sure that when they were playing it, neither Lord

Waterforde nor Clive would wonder why they were away for so long.

She hurried to her bedroom.

There as the *Duc* had promised her, was the veil that had been worn by many *Duchesses* de Sahran at their weddings.

Beside it were some of the precious jewels which she had discovered behind the Cascade.

The *Duc* had refused to show them to her until they were alone.

"They are for you, my Darling," he said, "because you brought them back to me. I want you to see them first, touch them first, and I want you to decide what you want to own personally."

"I am sure they are far too . . grand for . . me," Celita had said, thinking she might be overpowered by them.

"I would not let you have anything that would not add to your beauty," the *Duc* said. "It is very difficult to know how anybody could be more beautiful than you are now."

"Please go on thinking that," Celita said. "I shall be always frightened that those Ladies from Paris might lure you away from me because they know more about love than I do."

"I do not want you to know 'more about love' than I shall teach you," the *Duc* said. "And teaching you, my Lovely One, will be the most exciting, the most thrilling, and the most worthwhile thing I have ever done in my life."

He spoke with a deep sincerity which Celita found very moving.

She knew that with every word he spoke to her, and every time he touched her, he loved her more and more.

She might know very little about love, but at the same time she could not help being aware that to the *Duc* she was something exceptionally precious.

He therefore did not think of her in the same way as he thought of the other women with whom he had been enamoured.

Now as she saw the jewels waiting for her she wondered if he was going to make her a glittering bride.

As she picked up the first jewel that he had left for her she knew that only he could have been so perceptive.

To wear round her neck was a long diamond necklace which reached almost to her waist.

It was very simple and at the end of it was an exquisitely beautiful Cross.

It was set with large but very simply cut diamonds.

There was a very small tiara to wear over the veil on her head.

It was made in the form of small field-flowers – Forget-Me-Nots, Violets and Daisies.

It was so exquisitely set it could actually have been worn by a child.

But Celita understood why the *Duc* had chosen it for her and knew that nothing could be more becoming.

She put it on.

Then there was a bracelet, also of diamonds, from which hung quite a number of small Crosses.

She wondered who had collected them.

Then she saw that each one had a name and a date on the back of it.

She was sure she was right in thinking they were the dates when previous *Duchesses* de Sahran had been married.

She knew that the date of today with her name would be added to the bracelet.

There was nothing else.

'Only the *Duc*,' she thought, 'could have such exquisite taste and choose things which meant so much to both of them.'

She was determined as soon as they were married to become a Catholic so that they would worship together.

There was a knock on the door.

She knew that the *Vicomte* was waiting for her.

When she joined him he handed her a bouquet.

Again it was very simple, of white Lilies tied with a satin bow.

Celita knew the *Duc* had given it to her as a symbol of purity.

It was also the flower of the Mother of God whose name she bore.

Without saying anything the *Vicomte* drew her along the passage in which her bedroom was situated.

At the end there was a secondary staircase which led them to the back of the Château where the Chapel was situated.

When they drew near to it the *Vicomte* offered Celita his arm.

As they moved slowly onwards there was the sound of very soft music coming from an organ which was completely hidden.

The *Duc* was standing at the Altar steps.

His Private Chaplain was wearing the white vestments which were symbolic of Weddings and Christenings.

What Celita found very touching was that the *Duc* had had the whole Chapel decorated with Madonna Lilies.

They were on the Altar, against every wall, and in huge vases in the Chancel.

As they reached the *Duc*, he put out his hand to take hers and she saw the love in his eyes.

The Wedding Service started and Celita knew this was the perfect wedding for both of them.

Nothing could disturb or upset their happiness, and the future was theirs.

When the knelt for the Blessing, Celita felt as if they were both suddenly enveloped with a vivid light.

It did not come from the candles on the Altar.

She knew in her heart it was the light of love.

A light which came from the Divine and of which they were both aware when they prayed.

When the ceremony was over, without speaking the *Duc* took Celita up the stairs down which she had come with the *Vicomte*.

Gustav went away to join the others.

She knew that the *Duc's* plans had gone exactly as he intended.

She thought he would take her to his own room.

She was therefore surprised when he opened the door of the Master Suite which was at the end of the corridor.

They went into the great bed-room in which the *Duchesses* had slept for generations.

It was also decorated with Madonna Lilies.

There were lights burning each side of the huge four-poster bed with its gilded and carved posts and exquisitely decorated canopy of Cupids and Angels.

The *Duc* locked the door.

Then he said:

"My Darling, you are my wife. I can hardly believe that you are really mine, and I need no longer be afraid that I shall lose you, or that you will fall in love with someone else."

Celita gave a little laugh.

"I have had no opportunity of doing that!"

"And that is something which will never happen in the future," the *Duc* said.

Very gently he took off the little tiara of field-flowers and the diamond cross.

Then he was kissing her as he undid the back of her gown until it fell to the ground, with the soft rustle of a sigh.

Picking her up in his arms he carried her to the bed.

Lying with her head against the pillows she thought it was impossible for anyone to make a room more enchanting or more romantic.

She realised the *Duc* had left the curtains undrawn.

The casements were open so that they could see the stars which filled the sky.

Then before the *Duc* joined her he blew out the candles by the bed.

Now, which Celita had not noticed before, the moonlight came into the room with a silver light.

It seemed almost as if it came from Heaven itself.

The *Duc* put his arms round Celita.

"Have you enjoyed your Wedding, my Precious?" he asked.

"It has been wonderful. The most perfect, the most beautiful wedding any woman could have."

"It had to be perfect for you," he said, "because you are perfect. And now we start our perfect life together."

"I love .. you! I love .. you!" Celita said. "But, Darling, I am .. frightened!"

"Of me?" the *Duc* asked.

"Of course not! But in case you expect .. too much from me. You have thought of .. all this and made .. everything so utterly .. beautiful I could not .. bear you to be .. disappointed."

"Do you really think I could be disappointed?" the *Duc* asked, in a very deep voice. "I love you, and I swear to you this is true. I have never known love before. Of course, I have thought I was in love, but it was just an excitement and a physical satisfaction, which, like a delicious meal, is soon forgotten after one has eaten it."

"And what .. you feel .. for me really is .. different?" Celita asked.

"I love you, but I also worship you," the *Duc* said. "When you were married to me as *Mary* Celita I knew that your name would always be part of our marriage. I saw you holding the baby as Mary, the Mother of God, and that is how I think of you in my heart and in my soul."

"Oh, René! How could you say anything so marvellous?" Celita asked.

"I am trying to express in words what I feel in my mind and in my heart," he said. "That is what we must always do to each other, but you will have to help me."

"You know I .. will do .. anything .. you want," Celita said. "Anything to .. make you .. happy."

"I am ecstatically happy," the *Duc* said, "and I know that we have been guided and helped towards each other. Now there is so much for us both to do."

"That is what I want you to say," Celita said. "It is not . . only for . . horses, is it?"

The *Duc* shook his head.

"No, my Precious One, you have taught me that I am not only responsible for those who depend upon me here, but also for my country. There are things we must both do for France. But I cannot do them unless you help me."

"You know . . I will do . . that," Celita said. "But please . . Darling, love me and do not . . stop loving me."

"Do you think that is possible?" the *Duc* asked.

Then he was kissing her.

At first very gently and tenderly, as if she was infinitely precious and he was afraid of frightening her.

Then he felt her respond and her body moved against his.

He knew he had ignited in her the tiny flames of the fire which consumed him.

It was a fire that was spiritual as well as physical.

A fire which was like the light which had covered them in the Chapel and which was still in their souls.

Then as the *Duc* made Celita his, he knew they were one.

Not just for this life but for all Eternity.

ABOUT THE AUTHOR

Barbara Cartland, the world's most famous romantic novelist, who is also a historian, playwright, lecturer, political speaker and television personality, has now written over 589 books and sold over 600 million copies all over the world.

She has also had many historical works published and has written four autobiographies as well as the biographies of her mother and that of her brother, Ronald Cartland, who was the first Member of Parliament to be killed in the last war. This book has a preface by Sir Winston Churchill and has just been published with an introduction by the late Sir Arther Bryant.

"Love at the Helm" a novel written with the help and inspiration of the late Earl Mountbatten of Burma, Great Uncle of His Royal Highness The Prince of Wales, is being sold for the Mountbatten Memorial Trust.

She has broken the world record for the last nineteen years by writing an average of twenty-three books a year. In the Guiness Book of Records she is listed as the world's best-selling author.

Dame Barbara Cartland in 1978 sang an Album of Love Songs with the Royal Philharmonic orchestra.

In private life Barbara Cartland, who is a Dame of Grace of the Order of St.John of Jerusalem, Chairman of the St.John Council in Hertfordshire and Deputy President of the St.John Ambulance Brigade, has fought for better conditions and salaries for Midwives and Nurses.

She championed the cause for the Elderly in 1956 invoking a Government Enquiry into the "Housing Conditions of Old People".

In 1962 she had the Law of England changed so that Local Authorities had to provide camps for their own Gypsies. This has meant that since then thousands and thousands of Gypsy children have been able to go to School which they had never been able to do in the past, as their caravans were moved every twenty-four hours by the Police.

There are now fourteen camps in Hertfordshire and Barbara Cartland has her own Romany Gypsy Camp called Barbaraville by the Gypsies.

Her designs "Decorating with Love" are being sold all over the U.S.A. and the National Home Fashions League made her in 1981, "Woman of Achievement".

Barbara Cartland's book "Getting Older, Growing Younger" has been published in Great Britain and the U.S.A. and her fifth Cookery Book, "The Romance of Food" is now being issued by the House of Commons.

In 1984 she received at Kennedy Airport, America's Bishop Wright Air Industry Award for her contribution to the development of aviation. In 1931 she and two R.A.F. Officers thought of, and carried the first aeroplane-towed glider air-mail.

During the War she was Chief Lady Welfare Officer in Bedfordshire looking after 20,000 Service men and women. She thought of having a pool of Wedding Dresses at the War Office so a Service Bride could hire a gown for the day.

She bought 1,000 secondhand gowns without coupons for the A.T.S., the W.A.A.F.s and the W.R.E.N.S. In 1945 Barbara Cartland received the Certificate of Merit from Eastern Command.

In 1964 Barbara Cartland founded the National Association for Health of which she is the President, as a front for all the Health Stores and for any product made as alternative medicine.

This has now a £500,000,000 turnover a year, with one third going in export.

In January 1988 she received "La Medaille de Vermeil de la Ville to Paris" (the Gold Medal of Paris). This is the highest award to be given by the City of Paris for ACHIEVEMENT – 25 million books sold in France.

In March 1988 Barbara Cartland was asked by the Indian

Government to open their Health Resort outside Delhi. This is almost the largest Health Resort in the world.

Barbara Cartland was received with great enthusiasm by her fans, who also fêted her at a Reception in the city and she received the gift of an embossed plate from the Government.

Barbara Cartland was made a Dame of the Order of the British Empire in the 1991 New Year's Honours List, by Her Majesty The Queen, for her contribution to literature and for her work for the Community.

Dame Barbara had now written the greatest number of books by a British Author, passing the 564 books written by John Creasey.

AWARDS

1945   Receives Certificate of Merit, Eastern Command, for being Welfare Officer to 5,000 troops in Bedfordshire.

1953   Made a Commander of the Order of St.John of Jerusalem. Invested by H.R.H. The Duke of Gloucester at Buckingham Palace.

1972   Invested as Dame of Grace of the Order of St.John in London by The Lord Prior, Lord Cacia.

1981   Receives "Achiever of the Year" from the National Home Furnishing Association in Colorado Springs, U.S.A. for her designs for wallpaper and fabrics.

1984   Receives Bishop Wright Air Industry Award at Kennedy Airport, for inventing the aeroplane-towed Glider.

1988   Receives from Monsieur Chirac, The Prime Minister, The Gold Medal of the City of Paris, for selling 25 million books and giving a lot of employment.

1991   Invested as Dame of the Order of the British Empire, by H.M. The Queen at Buckingham Palace for her contribution to Literature.

STARS ORGANISATION SUPPORTING
ACTION FOR PEOPLE WITH
CEREBRAL PALSY

A SPECIAL THANK YOU FROM
CAROL M MYER MBE, DIRECTOR

STARS ORGANISATION SUPPORTING ACTION FOR
PEOPLE WITH CEREBRAL PALSY

The SOS is delighted to be associated with Jim Martin's 'Home Shopping Direct' and Cartland Promotions. For every copy of 'Fascination in France' that is claimed, the SOS will receive a small donation from both companies. This money will go towards our Children's Project.

We are currently working with the Spastics Society to establish 100 'Schools for Parents' where parents can work alongside their pre school children, aged 0 - 5, developing movement skills like walking, feeding and toileting. Our aim is to give opportunity to children with disability so they can integrate with their friends in school and play.

Cerebral palsy is a disability for life - there is no cure but with help in the early years the effects of this disability can be reduced.

The SOS is committed to funding the equipment for these centres. It costs £500 to purchase equipment for one child and £10,000 to equip a centre. We are so grateful to Jim Martin's 'Home Shopping Direct' and Cartland Promotions for supporting The SOS. I hope you will support us too.

Carol M Myer, M.B.E.
Director
The SOS